THE
BLUE
MESA

THE
BLUE
MESA

A
NOVEL

OLIVIA
GODAT

atmosphere press

For my grandchildren:
Jared, Zach, Kylie, and Jason

PROLOGUE
1664

IN GRATITUDE FOR services he performed for the Crown, Don Rafael Montez was given a land grant signed by King Philip IV, and in the year of our Lord, 1664, he led his people from Mexico for more than seven hundred leagues to settle in the land called *Nueva Mejico*.

On horseback and on foot, by oxcart and mule-drawn wagons, the colonists plodded alongside the Rio Grande. Vaqueros herded the cattle and horses. Shepherds, with the help of nimble and well-trained dogs, tended the sheep. Young boys with long sticks prodded the skinny swine along the path.

Doña Isabella, heavy with child, sat on a padded seat in a carriage pulled by a team of matching black horses. Her handmaid, Marta, rode in the carriage with her, arranging pillows, offering sips of water, and brushing road dust from her blue-gray traveling dress.

One evening, as the pilgrims rested beside the lower

reaches of the Rio Grande, a Tejas Indian stumbled into camp. He knelt at Isabella's feet and kissed the hem of her blue gown. Speaking in a strange tongue, the Indian held up a square of rawhide on which a likeness of a woman wearing a blue dress had been painted.

Rafael stepped forward with his loaded musket in one hand and his sharpened dagger in the other and said, "Stay away from my lady."

Old Pedro, their guide, had traveled the Royal Road many times as guard and as guide and knew the language and ways of the native people. He lifted a restraining hand. "The man means no harm," Old Pedro said. "That painting is a picture of *La Dama de Azul*. The Lady in Blue once gave his father a rosary as a token of her existence, but she has not appeared before his people in many years. This man has never seen her and he believes that Doña Isabella is the Blue Lady."

"No," she said. "That cannot be."

The Blue Lady had been a devout Spanish nun whose order dressed in blue habits. Day after day she knelt in prayer for guidance to bring the Word of the Lord to the heathens of the New World. Legend says that her prayers were so intense and her belief so strong that, although she never left her convent cell in Spain, her spirit traveled to New Mexico where she entreated the Indians to listen to the dark-robed men she would send to teach them the Holy Faith. The Indians so respected the nun they called the Blue Lady that they welcomed the missionaries as her disciples.

The painting on the rawhide did carry a slight resemblance to Doña Isabella; still, she did not want to be thought of as that holy woman, the Blue Lady.

The Tejas Indian spoke. Isabella did not understand his words but she heard the pleading in his voice, saw the poverty in his eyes, smelled the hunger on his breath.

"This man is starved for more than salvation, Rafael," she said. "Give him enough food to fill his belly and that of his people."

In respect of his wife's wishes, he gave the Indian generous gifts: a fat steer, a sack of beans, two she-goats with kids by their sides, and sent the man on his way. Smoke signals and drum beats carried the message across the land: "The Blue Lady comes."

Hidden in rock crevices and behind trees, the dark-eyed people of the Pueblo Nation followed every move the colonists made as they trudged through the dusty countryside.

The natives of that area were familiar with the men who had hair on their faces and wore shiny coats, and they knew of the cruelty of those men. Many an Indian had felt the sharp prick of the sword and carried the whip scars on his back. They obeyed the force of the soldiers but did not trust those men who rode swiftly across the land on *caballos*, the only word the Indians knew for horse as their own tongue had no expression for the animal.

They trusted only the Blue Lady, and they vowed to guard and protect her and her people. Not once were the colonists attacked by Indians. Not even the marauding Apache or Navajo dared approach their camp, and the settlers traveled the Royal Road confident the conquistadors had indeed conquered the Indian Nation.

Days later, Old Pedro galloped up to Don Rafael and said, "There it is, Señor." He pointed north where heat waves danced on a distant blue mesa.

Rafael consulted his map and turned to Gaspar, his *mayordomo*. "He's right, Gaspar. That mesa is our landmark." He made a wide circling gesture with his arm. "All this, as far as you can see and beyond, is the land that our good king granted us. Tell the people we are home and to set up camp until we can build our houses." He rode to the carriage where his wife waited.

Sweat beaded her upper lip, fatigue shadowed her amber eyes, her travel-stained blue dress stretched tight across her pregnant belly, but to him she was beautiful as the day they met. With a courtly bow, he handed her out of the carriage.

"Come, my dear," he said. "Come see our new land where we will make our home." With his arm around her waist, he showed her the sweeping valley, the rugged plains.

"It looks to be a good land, Rafael," she said.

"We will build our house over there beneath that stand of piñon for shade from the afternoon sun," he said, "and we will build the patio to face the west so we can watch the morning sun paint the snowy mountain tops pink.

"Our fields will reach to the river, and there on the edge of the valley I will build a guardhouse. Old Pedro tells me the Apache live to the south and attack settlers often. I will stock the guardhouse like a garrison and this I pledge to you, my wife, my love, that I will make this land a safe home for you and our children."

He kissed her cheek and returned to his duties. He ordered that a feast be prepared and sent men into the forest for game. The hunters returned to the camp with four wild turkeys and a fat doe. Women plucked the turkeys and stowed the feathers in a bag for future use.

They stuffed the cavities with wild onion and sage that one of the women had gathered and placed the turkeys on spits over the fire. Saul Guzman, cobbler and saddle maker, skinned the deer with care and folded the hide, hair side out. He would tan the hide later. He cut the deer meat into thin strips. Some, the women cooked for the feast, the remainder they salted for drying in the sun.

Chief Leaping Antelope and his band of warriors had no interest in the food preparations. Their interest was the woman wearing the blue dress. Patiently they waited for the Blue Lady to appear. When a settler passed, at times near enough to touch, the watchers flattened their bodies and blended with the earth and the rocks and the trees.

Rafael asked Gaspar to open a cask of wine in celebration and the people ate and drank, talked and laughed, sang and danced. The coyotes howled their nightly serenade and, tired from the long trip, the settlers retired to their pallets. The summer breeze whispered through the cottonwoods and the answering murmur of the river soothed the weary travelers.

While the camp slept, Chief Leaping Antelope and his unseen band of Cucuri kept vigil over the Blue Lady.

The moon rose and the night glimmered in a soft light. Doña Isabella felt the first birth pangs and slipped out of bed. She stood a moment and stroked her unborn child with circular motions. With her hands pressed against her back, she paced around the campfire. Suddenly she stopped and, with a gasp, bent over clutching her belly.

Chief Leaping Antelope whispered to Little Turtle, one of his warriors, "The Blue Lady is ready to give birth. Take two of the Spaniards' ponies. Be very quiet but ride with the wind and bring my wife, Morning Star." He watched as Little Turtle silently sprang on the back of one of the horses and leading another, galloped away. The pueblo was poor, and like their own Blue Corn Woman, the Blue Lady's blessing would ensure a bountiful harvest.

Isabella awakened Marta and she called for the midwife, Dorotea, who had birthed many babies. They curtained a wagon with blankets and covered a stack of sheepskins with silken sheets for the birthing bed.

Don Rafael strode to the wagon, his eyes shaded with worry. "What's going on?" he asked.

"Nothing to be concerned about, Señor. It is the Señora's time. Her baby is about to be born," Marta said and waved her hand. "Go now, this is women's work, but we will need light."

"Gaspar," he shouted, "bring torches." And soon the birthing wagon blazed with light.

At Isabella's soft moan Rafael leaped into the wagon. "Isabella, *querida*, you're in pain. I'm so sorry. I didn't realize." With his kerchief he wiped sweat from her face. He stroked her auburn hair and murmured words of love. At the next pain Isabella clutched his hand. Her nails bit into his skin, but he did not flinch.

Dorotea gave him a knotted length of cloth that she had tied to the wagon seat. "Let her pull on this when the pains come, Señor. Now you must go. We will bring the baby to you."

"No. I will not leave my wife." He lifted Isabella and held her between his knees, her head on his lap.

The women glanced at one another. Never had such a thing happened. Men did not witness childbirth. Marta shrugged. No one could tell the *patrón* what to do.

Many hours later Dorotea whispered so Don Raphael

could not hear, "Things are very bad, Marta. There are two babies, they are not lying right in the womb and the señora is very weak. I have never done it before, but I will have to cut her womb open to save the babies."

"No," Marta said, "if you do, the señora will surely die."

Dorotea's old face crumpled with sorrow. "If I don't, they all will die."

"Is there nothing else?"

"Prayers," Dorotea said. "We can pray."

"*Madre de Dios.*" Marta stumbled out of the wagon and fell to her knees moaning, "Ay! Ay! Ay!"

Gaspar grasped her shoulder. "What is it, woman?"

Marta told him Isabella was near death and, as one, the Spaniards dropped to their knees uttering prayers to the Blessed Mother.

Gaspar turned at the sound of hoof beats. A tall Indian with graying hair strode into camp leading a horse that carried a woman. Gaspar pulled out his sword. "Those horses belong to us. Dismount at once and we will allow you to leave in peace." All the men stood beside him with drawn swords ready to do battle. The Indian raised his hand. "We have come in peace. I am Leaping Antelope, Summer Chief of the Cucuri Pueblo of the Tewa Tribe, and this is my wife Morning Star. She is the 'umbilical cord cutting mother' for our pueblo and is here to help the Blue Lady."

Gaspar's black beard jutted out. "There is no Blue Lady here," he said, his brown eyes glittering with a ferocious light. "Go away and do not return. We have no quarrel with you." The men formed a single line barring the Indians' path. The women huddled behind them. A child whimpered and was quickly hushed.

Morning Star slid off her horse. "I've seen many births such as this, and I can help the Blue Lady."

"I will allow no one to go near my mistress," Gaspar said. "We have vowed to protect our mistress to the death."

Then Marta stepped forward. "Let her try and help," she said. "We've done all we can." She turned to Morning Star. "Please help my lady. She is in danger of losing her life and that of the two babies."

Gaspar shook his sword at Morning Star. "Remember what I say. No harm will come to my mistress."

Carrying her medicine bag, Morning Star brushed past him. "I'd as soon cut off my hand as harm the Blue Lady." She climbed into the wagon and said, "Everyone leave us, except you," she pointed to Dorotea, "you may stay and help." Then she turned to Rafael. "You must go, Señor, men are not needed at this time."

Rafael did not look up. "I will not leave my wife."

Morning Star shook her head, mumbled a few prayers of her own and said, "Very well, Señor. I don't have time to argue, but you are not to interfere. Help her drink this." She handed him a clay bowl that held a liquid with an odd odor.

"What is it?"

"Nothing that will harm her, only something to help her relax while I turn the babies in her womb."

The morning sun had peeked through purple rain clouds floating across a pale sky by the time Don Rafael stepped out of the wagon, a white bundle in each arm. His eyes were dark with fatigue but he smiled. "Doña Isabella is resting and all are well. What is the date, Gaspar?"

"July 25, Señor, the feast day of Saint James."

Don Rafael presented the swaddled baby in his right arm. "This child shall be named Diego."

Thunder rolled and lightning flashed. The baby wailed.

"He's been touched by the Holy Spirit," a man said.

"He will grow strong and brave," said another.

"A soldier of Santiago," Gaspar shouted and brandished his sword.

Don Rafael extended his left arm. "And this one shall be named Estrella in honor of Morning Star." The baby flicked her eyes open, yawned and shut her eyes. The sun peeked from behind a storm cloud and threw a rainbow across the pewter sky.

"She has been blessed by the angels," a woman said.

"She will grow beautiful and gracious," said another.

"A great lady," Marta said and kissed the baby's curled fist.

Don Rafael walked around the camp and showed his children to each person. He stopped in front of Chief Leaping Antelope. "I have no words to thank you, all your people, and especially your wife, Morning Star, for your help. What can I do to repay you? Whatever I have is yours. If you ever need help, I will be at your side."

"All we want is the lady's blue dress."

"My wife's blue dress?"

"Yes."

Rafael asked no further questions. "Marta, bring Doña Isabella's blue dress."

Marta brought the dress and Rafael placed the babies in her arms. He clicked his heels, bowed and passed the dress to Chief Leaping Antelope. The chief heaved a sigh of relief, took his knife, cut the dress into strips and handed one to each member of the pueblo. They each tied a ribbon around their heads and shuffled around the campfire in a dance of thanksgiving. Chief Leaping Antelope said that now the Blue Corn Woman would smile upon their pueblo. She would send the rains, their crops would grow, and they would prosper once again.

A gentle rain began to fall. The Cucuri lifted their faces to the sky and chanted prayers of thanks to the gods for the Blue Lady and her two children.

They called the boy child Storm Cloud and the girl baby Rainbow.

CHAPTER 1
1680

I BRUSHED MY shirt sleeve across my face and told myself it was the smoke that brought the water to my eyes. I am sixteen years old, a man, and men do not weep. My name is Diego Francisco de Montez y Montera. It is a good name, a name that I bear with pride. For many centuries my ancestors fought to protect our mother country from the invading Moorish infidels.

The battle cry "Santiago" has echoed throughout New Mexico for over one hundred and fifty years. With a heavy heart, I realize that the battle cry will ring no more. Like us, the soldiers are fleeing for their lives.

We retrace the path my parents trod sixteen years ago to settle in New Mexico, the trail forged by the courageous conquistadors. I pray that I can be as brave while I lead my people south along the *Camino Real* and to safety at *El Paso del Norte*.

There are not so many of us. All our Indian servants

vanished many days ago. The shepherds, Juan and Lopé, took our sheep into the deep canyons. Gaspar managed to save his fighting roosters and some of the other fowl. The Indians ran off most of the remaining livestock. We are thankful to escape with our lives. My father lies near death in a wagon next to the wounded vaquero, Clemente. Old Pedro—dead. Estrella—I do not know where my twin sister is.

A strange thing happened after I rescued her from the Apache, and it is difficult to believe, but I have the proof here in my pocket. To better understand it, I will write my story from the very beginning as we travel south to safety.

CHAPTER 2

FOR US, THE Pueblo War started the morning of my patron saint's feast day. My father and I were returning from the sheep camp. We received word that once again the Navajos had raided our sheep camp, so we had ridden to the mesa to investigate. The long drought had dried up many of the Indians' crops, game was scarce, and on the edge of famine, they raided the ranchers' livestock often. The Navajo usually stole sheep, and the Apache had a fondness for horses and cattle, but either one would steal whichever animal presented the least difficulty.

Although the plundering of the ranch affected us, we did nothing about it. "Why do we allow this thievery of our livestock?" I asked Father. "Why don't we put a stop to it?"

"I've spent too many years as a soldier and seen too much bloodshed. Now I want to live in peace. I will not fight the Indians over the livestock, Diego. A few animals are not worth the loss of one human life. If we do not retaliate, the Indians won't attack our home."

He was right. We had many friends among the Pueblo Indians and did not endure the bloodthirsty Indian attacks some of the other ranchers in the Rio Grande Valley suffered.

Father pointed to the sparse yellow and tan grass. "This drought has lasted much too long."

The wind swirled eddies of red dust in an arroyo that carried floodwaters in the rainy season. The air crackled with dry lightning. Far to the west, scant pockets of snow lay scattered in the high valleys, lightning bolts danced on the cloud-hooded peaks. "There's rain in the mountains."

"That is good. The runoff will fill the river, and we can irrigate our crops, but it will do little for the plains."

From the corner of my eye, I caught movement and turned my gaze to the hillside. Indians slipped between trees and behind rocks. "Indians! Maybe they are the ones who stole the sheep."

"Pay no attention to them and keep riding. Navajo stole the sheep. These are Apache, probably scouting for game and not interested in war. There are only five of them."

We recognized the Indians as Apache from the way they sat in the saddle, which was only a sheepskin strapped on with rawhide. They learned to ride after we Spaniards introduced the horse to the new world a little over one hundred years ago, and they are excellent horsemen.

An arrow whined over our heads, and we galloped for the dry wash. Before the horses had skidded to a stop in the bottom of the arroyo, Father and I were on our bellies readying our weapons amid the flying dust and pebbles.

Father had a musket from his days as a conquistador, as well as a bow, which he used alternately with his musket, but my only weapon was a bow.

Four of the Apache raced toward us shooting a steady stream of arrows. We waited until they were within one hundred yards before we returned the volley. When Father's musket boomed, the Indians danced their horses out of range and held a conference.

With a mighty war whoop, they rushed us in a marvelous display of horsemanship. They hooked a foot in a rawhide loop braided in their horses' manes, and with their mustangs at a full gallop, shot arrows from underneath their ponies' bellies and necks. The fifth Apache raced his spotted mustang toward us. He hurled his lance. It landed upright in the dirt, quivering not two paces from my boot heel.

Father shot his musket again and the blast stopped the Indians. With defiant shouts, they swooped down to pick up their spent arrows and galloped away.

Father stood and brushed the dust from his trousers. "You conducted yourself well, Diego."

Impressed by the Indians' feats of horsemanship and concentrating on my aim, I'd had no thoughts of danger, and only regretted that I hadn't so much as wounded an Apache.

But Father said, "The Apache warrior is not to be taken lightly. If they had been serious, they would have kept us pinned down in the arroyo until no breath of life remained in our bodies. We were never in any danger."

I pulled the lance from the dirt and examined it. "I think the one who threw this was Black Bear, Father. I'm sure that he rides that brown and white pony."

He shrugged and said, "I don't think he'd do something like that. We've known Black Bear since he was a child."

I was not convinced, however, that the Apache meant us no harm. I had never told Father of Black Bear's resentment toward us.

When we were younger, Black Bear, White Wolf, and I had been constant companions and had pledged to take the blood oath of loyalty to one another. But on the planned day, Black Bear said, "I will not mingle my blood with that of a Spaniard."

"Come on, Black Bear," White Wolf said. "We're all three friends, aren't we? We vowed to take the blood oath and go on our quest together."

"It's all right for you, White Wolf, you're a Cucuri of the Tewa, but I am an Apache." Black Bear lifted his chin and crossed his sinewy arms on his breast.

"What difference does that make?" White Wolf said. "You were an Apache when you came to live with us. Nothing has changed since we made the vow."

"I didn't know then how I came to live with you, but now I know that if not for the Spaniards, I'd be with my own people."

"Who told you that?" I asked. "I've never done anything to you."

"The elders have told me stories of how many of our brave warriors met their deaths in battles with the Spaniards. And they have told me how the Spanish priests have hung and whipped medicine men of the Tewa, burned their prayer sticks and filled the kivas with sand. I am telling you this, White Wolf, because even if you don't believe me, you should know these things. Already your People of the Sun are planning revenge. But go both of you.

Go find your vision and take your foolish blood oath. And then, someday, White Wolf, you will come to understand that no Spaniard is ever a friend of an Indian, no matter the tribe." His shoulders stiff and head held high, Black Bear had walked away from us.

Although White Wolf and I remained the best of friends, Black Bear never again visited our ranch.

For the rest of the ride home, I kept a close watch on the mesa tops for any Indian sign.

When we arrived home, a troop of soldiers met us in the meadow that spread in front of our house.

"To what do we owe the honor of your visit, captain?" my father asked.

"We are on patrol, and it is our duty to inform you and all the out-lying ranchers that the Pueblo Indians are planning to rebel against Spanish rule."

"We have never had any problems with the Indians," Father said. "What has happened that they are planning a rebellion at this time?"

"Nothing of consequence, sir. When they disobey, we must punish them. Then they become insolent and make threats. This has happened many times before, but our spies tell us that now the entire Pueblo Nation is rising against us, and the governor insisted that we warn the citizens."

"Thank you for the information," Father said, "but I'm not worried. The Indians have always been our friends."

"Hah!" The captain snorted and wiped his sleeve across his nose. "The Indians don't know about friendship."

Father's gray eyes turned cold as a winter snow cloud. "The Tewa are our friends."

"Maybe, but we find that the Indians do not appreciate

all we do for them. We teach them to plant and grow corn, and they steal the harvest from us. Most of them are thieves, by the way, and then complain when we cut off their left hand. It does no good to flog them for their sins."

In a voice hard as hailstones, Father said, "Perhaps if you practiced human kindness, the Indians would be more agreeable to your teachings."

The captain shrugged. "We tried that. At the urging of the priests, our previous governor arrested forty-seven medicine men. After all, they were little more than devil worshippers and sorcerers. Of course, they had to be punished. They understand only the whip, but some had to be hung. Our present governor released the prisoners, but they didn't appreciate it. Popé, a strong and important medicine man from Taos preached against us and united the Pueblos, together with their sworn enemies the Apache and the Navajo. Now they have declared war on us, and all Spaniards are in danger.

"You are welcome to bring your family to the garrison in Santa Fe if you change your mind about the Indians. Many of the other ranchers have already taken their families there to safety."

"Thank you, captain, but we have nothing to fear from the Indians. They are our friends, and we have our own guard house." Father pointed to the rock tower that stood at the base of the hill and protected our hacienda from the southeast. "Now if you'll excuse me, my son and I have tasks we must attend to."

"Well, I have warned you. I understand you have a pretty, young daughter. The Indians want Spanish girls for wives and have already kidnapped two, but it's nothing to me what you do. Keep a sharp lookout because we won't be back until we have this uprising under control." The captain turned his horse and shouted to his men. They trooped up the hill and out of sight.

I heard the lonesome call of the mourning dove, and a sense of foreboding tickled the back of my neck.

CHAPTER 3

BECAUSE IT WAS our special day, that afternoon, Father allowed my twin sister, Estrella, to ride the mesa with me, and she wanted to race our horses.

I learned my riding skills from Gaspar, who has been with Father since their days as conquistadors. When I was a young child Gaspar placed me in front of him, and I would hold on to the horse's mane as he chased the long-horned cattle. When I was five years old, Gaspar gave me my first horse, a skittish brown and white mustang. Frequently the horse caught me leaning the wrong way when a jackrabbit startled him, so I often had bruises after I hit the rocky ground. Gaspar gave me no sympathy, but a lot of advice, and I soon learned to ride any horse on the ranch. By the time I was ten years old I was riding with the vaqueros. Estrella had to learn to ride on a gentle pony.

I galloped my black horse across the mesa top brandishing my new sword and shouting "Santiago." My father said I was now a man, and I received the sword for my birthday. It was a fine sword, made of Toledo steel with a handle and hilt of silver and brass, worthy of any brave conquistador. Mula, my heavy-footed horse, crashed through the sagebrush, and his big hooves pounded the dirt as he ran.

I heard Estrella scream, and from the corner of my eye saw her bay mare racing without a rider down the mesa. I reined Mula to a stop.

Estrella stood staring at the ground, the only movement the slight breeze fanning her skirts against her legs. Her new star sapphire pendant, she had received for her birthday, glittered in the sun. "What do you see, Star?" I called out.

Estrella made no sound. She pointed a shaky finger to the ground.

I leaned from my horse and saw the coiled snake, its tail rattling and forked tongue flicking toward my sister. I didn't stop to think. I grabbed the rawhide lariat from my saddle and lashed out, beating the rattlesnake again and again. I sprang from the horse and with my sword, skewered the rattler through its belly. I held the sword over my head like a standard. On the tip, the snake writhed and squirmed, its mouth hung open and its fangs dripped deadly venom.

"There, Estrella, that's one snake that won't bother you again." I wouldn't say I was afraid exactly, but my breath came hard and fast.

"How'd you know to whip that snake with the rope?" Estrella asked, her eyes wide with fear, or maybe excitement. Estrella liked excitement and usually managed to find some.

"The vaqueros taught me. Esteban gave me the reata. He made it special for me and showed me how to lasso cattle by the horns." I remembered when Esteban made the rope. A cow had been butchered for meat, and with an awl, Esteban attached the hide to a knot in a piñon tree. Using the awl to gauge the size, he turned the cowhide into a single string by drawing the hide around the edge of his knife. Then he scraped off the hair. After soaking and stretching the rawhide strings he braided them into a rope. When that was done, he had soaked and stretched the rope again and rubbed tallow on it. Esteban told me I must grease the rope often to keep it pliable. "I saw Bonita running down the mesa. What happened?"

"She reared when she heard the rattlesnake, and I couldn't hold on. She didn't mean to throw me, and I'm not hurt."

Estrella had to ride sidesaddle, so I could see how it happened. "Climb up behind me," I told her. "We better get home. Although Father doesn't say so, he's worried about the Indian war, and he'll come looking for us when Bonita shows up at the stable. But you'll have to ride astride."

"I don't mind." Estrella reached out her hand and I helped her mount up behind me.

With the sharp dusty scent of sage all around us, we headed for home. We didn't get very far before Father on his gray stallion galloped toward us. His war-horse, El Cid, is old and out to pasture now. For years, Father mated the old stallion with the finest mares in an effort to breed a horse as strong and brave as El Cid. Father claims this young stallion is almost as fine a horse and is called El Cid the Second. "What happened, children? Are you all right?"

"A snake frightened Bonita and she threw me. I'm not hurt, and Diego killed the snake, Papa."

Father looked at me and frowned at the snake wriggling on the tip of my sword. "What do you plan to do with that rattlesnake, Son?"

"I'm taking it to Saul Guzman and have him skin it for me." Everyone knew that Saul Guzman brought his family to the New World to escape the Inquisition Cells of Spain. No one spoke of it though for fear word would reach the authorities.

Estrella tittered behind her hand, but Father only shrugged. "Hurry home, then. Your mother is worried." He turned his horse down the mesa.

"I know why you want Saul Guzman to skin the rattler," Estrella whispered.

Estrella almost never whispered, so I should have known better, but I asked anyway. "Why?"

"You just want an excuse to see Rebecca."

My face grew hot. "Why do you say that?"

"You like her. I know you do, and I know something you don't."

"What? What do you know?" I knew my face turned red as the cactus flowers that dotted the desert.

Estrella pressed her nose into my back and giggled. "I'm not going to tell you."

"You're a tease, Estrella. You better hang on because I'm going to race Mula down the hill, and if you fall off it won't be my fault." I touched the horse with the big rowels on my spurs and Mula broke into a bone-jarring trot. I stood in the stirrups to absorb the shock, but Estrella bounced from side to side and up and down.

"All right, I'm sorry," Estrella said in short stuttering

gasps. "I didn't mean anything. I like Rebecca too. She's my best friend in the entire world."

I reined the horse to an easy stride. "Anyway, I want Saul to make me a hatband. The snake is pretty. See?" Grinning, I waved the sword at her. No longer writhing, the snake hung limp, jaws slack, its eyes hooded.

Estrella shuddered and drew away. "Maybe you think it's pretty, but I won't touch that thing."

I chuckled. "Come on, Estrella. It won't hurt you. It's dead. See?"

"You're mean, Diego. You're only trying to get back at me. You win, all right?" Laughing, we rode down the mesa.

The scent of bread baking filled the air as we approached the courtyard, and my mouth watered. With a long handled wooden paddle, Marta our cook, pulled loaves of bread and cinnamon-flavored cookies from the *horno*—a clay oven heated with piñon wood and brushed clean of ash before used for baking.

Both Mother and Marta waited for us by the water well. Father had his arm around Mother and had told them about the rattlesnake.

"You can see for yourself, *querida,* the children are all right." A long time ago Marta told us that our parents acted like this, always touching, kissing, and calling each other sweet names, because they loved each other so much. At times it made me feel special somehow, but other times it embarrassed me.

"Ay! Ay! Ay!" wailed Marta. "What am I to do?" She fanned her face with the corner of her shawl.

"What is it, Marta? Are you all right?" Mother asked.

Marta turned to Father. "That little minx, Estrella, is

riding astride showing her petticoats. How am I ever to make a lady out of that young miss if you allow her to ride around in that manner?"

Father chuckled. "Riding astride won't hurt the girl, and it's safer. If she had a regular saddle, Bonita would never have thrown her. You might think about making a divided skirt for Estrella so she can ride without showing her underwear."

"Señor! I'm shocked! How can you say such a thing?"

Father grinned. "What do you think, Isabella? Is Marta shocked because I suggested a divided skirt for Estrella or because I said 'underwear'?"

Marta muttered and called upon all the saints in heaven to preserve her and her charges from unseemly conduct.

Mother patted Marta's arm. "It's all right, Marta. He's only teasing, and we have plenty of time to teach Estrella the ways of a lady."

Behind me, Estrella shook with silent laughter. I knew if I looked at her, neither one of us could keep from laughing out loud. Poor Marta, after living all those years in New Mexico, she insisted that Estrella and I behave in the manner of ladies and gentlemen of Old Spain. But Marta's been with us since before we were born and she is much loved by us all.

At the piñon log corral, the vaquero, Esteban, asked, "What do you have there, young man?" Six years older than I, he had the bone structure and coloring of his Aztec grandmother. He wore his black hair in a single braid tied with a leather strip.

"I'm going to ask Saul Guzman to make a hatband for me."

"I'll take care of Mula for you. Guzman is over there." Esteban pointed. "Ask him to save the meat for me after he skins it, and I'll have it for dinner."

"You eat snake?" Estrella asked.

"Sure, why not? I'll cut it in pieces and roast it over the fire. It tastes good, once you get past the idea of it being a snake."

"Well, you can have my share." Estrella laughed and went in search of Rebecca.

"Will you try it, Diego?" asked Esteban.

"Well...I guess so. You say it tastes good?" I greatly admired the vaquero and wanted to be like him.

"I think it's possible that maybe some time you'll have to learn to eat whatever the land has to offer." Esteban laughed. "But don't worry, we have plenty of cows and sheep. There are deer and turkeys in the forest, so it will be a long time before you'll have to eat snake."

"If you cook it, I'll eat it." If Esteban ate snake, so would I. "Now I have to go see Saul." At the piñon-log tanning shed I talked to Saul about making a hatband.

Guzman agreed and said, "Leave the hat with me, Diego. I'll have the hatband ready by this evening. Snakeskin dries quickly and is easy to shape."

He slashed the snake down the belly from throat to tail and stripped back the skin as though from a grape. The peeled snake lay coiled on the table like a long gray sausage.

I handed Saul my hat and ran my hand over my head. I'd become accustomed to my leather sombrero and felt undressed without it. I wrapped my yellow cotton kerchief around my head and knotted it at the nape.

CHAPTER 4

AS I WALKED out the door, I saw Estrella and Rebecca walking toward me.

"White Wolf is here to see you, Diego," Rebecca said. "He's waiting down by the cornfield." She was no longer the playmate of my childhood, but a woman with the beauty of the cactus flower and a voice like music on the wind. I had never told her how I felt about her, how my heart beat faster and how I found it difficult to breathe in her presence.

The three of us hurried to the cornfield where White Wolf stood talking to Pedro. The small, thin man, too old for any heavy work, acts as the lookout for Indian trouble. He sits all day long in a brush and reed shelter at the edge of the cornfield and occupies and amuses himself by slinging rocks at crows and rabbits that invade the crops. Sometimes he gets lucky and knocks a cottontail on the head, then he has rabbit stew for dinner.

Always polite, White Wolf greeted us by our Indian names, "Hello, Storm Cloud, Rainbow, and Rebecca. Your father, he is well, I hope. And the Blue Lady enjoys good health?"

"Yes, thank you, White Wolf. It's good to see you." White Wolf, only a year older than I, has been my friend my entire life. He was seated on the ground talking to the old man, and we greeted each other with our secret handshake.

Old Pedro was the teller of tales for our hacienda and he told us the same story many times over, "so you won't forget it," he said. He told us stories of the first settlers and their hardships, and of the politicians, soldiers, and priests who marched into New Mexico for gold, and glory, and God.

Old Pedro peered at us through his red-rimmed eyes. "I suppose you're all here for a story. Sit down then, all of you, and today I will tell you the story of El Dorado."

White Wolf and I glanced at each other and smiled; we'd heard most of his stories many times. We all sat on the ground, Rebecca so close to me, my skin tingled where our thighs touched.

"All Spaniards should know about El Dorado," Old Pedro said and began his tale. "It all started long, long ago when the Moors were still in possession of Spain, but my story begins when the Spaniards first came to the New World."

My pulse raced when Rebecca peeked at me through her eyelashes and smiled. I was grateful I knew the story because I couldn't concentrate on it. I could think only of Rebecca and her sparkling blue eyes and long golden braid. I picked up a stick and traced lines in the dirt while the old man talked.

"Many years ago," Old Pedro said, "a valiant Spaniard by the name of Cabeza de Vaca was shipwrecked on the coast of Mexico far to the south of here. The natives captured him, made him a slave, and brought him here to New Mexico. Now, this man who called himself "Head of a Cow" had a very quick wit. He learned the languages of the different pueblos, and his cunning in trading so impressed the Indians they allowed de Vaca more freedom than they generally permitted a slave.

"One day he heard two women discussing Cibola. The legend of the Seven Cities of Gold is one which is known to all Spaniards. A long time ago, in the year 714, Don Rodrigo of Spain lost his kingdom to the Muhamadans. Some say that it was in the year 1150 in the city of Merida. No matter." Old Pedro made a dismissive gesture with his hand.

"In either case, seven devout bishops refused to obey the infidel Moors and fled across the ocean. Each bishop established his own city and accumulated great wealth. No one ever knew where these cities made of gold were located, but all knew the seven were grouped together.

"Escape never far from his mind, de Vaca determined that when he did escape he'd come back to this beautiful country to find Cibola. The seven bishops could find no better place in which to establish their kingdoms than in this enchanted land."

Old Pedro took a sip of water from his flask and continued with his story. "De Vaca did escape, and after seven years of wandering naked, barefoot, and starving, he stumbled into Mexico City. There, he told wonderful stories of this land of many lands and the people who lived here. He told of cattle with great humps on their backs that roamed the plains, of the delicious fat dogs roasted on spits, and of the tuna—the round, flat cactus buds that when peeled were a delight to eat. He told of cities that gleamed and sparkled in the sunlight.

"The viceroy of Mexico outfitted expedition after expedition to search for Cibola, the Seven Cities of Gold, and to bring Christianity to the heathens. Instead of El Dorado, they found only poor Indian villages. Pueblos. That is why the Indian tribes living in this area came to be known as 'Pueblo Indians.'

"Try as they might, even the missionaries failed in their efforts to bring the true faith to the unbelievers. The Pueblo Indians turned against them. They burned the missions. They killed the priests. They destroyed the homes of the early colonists and stole their horses and cattle. For almost forty years the Spaniards lived in peril."

Pedro lifted his head, looked at us and beamed. "But the brave conquistadors protected the settlers and this land. I, myself, fought many a battle with the Indians.

"Although we have never found the yellow metal, we have something much better than gold. We here in the Rio Grande Valley have prosperous farms and are safe from the Pueblo Indians." After he finished the story, Old Pedro took another sip of water from the leather water flask slung across his shoulders.

We all thanked him and rose to our feet. "Come on, White Wolf," I said. "Let's go pick up my hat."

"I want to see it too," Estrella said.

I glanced at Rebecca and smiled. "Do you want to come with us?"

She nodded and slipped her hand in mine and we laced

our fingers. We didn't speak. My mind was filled with her nearness, her scent, her touch, and I could think of nothing to say. White Wolf and Estrella walked behind us to the tanning shed, heads together, whispering.

Saul had cut off the rattles and curled the snakeskin around my hat with its tail caught in its mouth. He attached leather strings on the hat so I could tie it under my chin.

CHAPTER 5

FATHER HAD INVITED the entire Cucuri Pueblo for a feast in honor of our birthday. He was talking with Chief Leaping Antelope and a group of men when we arrived at the house.

"Our medicine man, Lame Deer, has not returned from the Tsin," the chief said. "Two moons ago he went to the sacred mesa to pray, and now I am concerned for him."

"He'll not return. The wind that blows through the tunnels of the mesa carried him away, and we will never see him again. Lame Deer knew the risk when he went there to pray. I warned him of the danger and made a charm to protect him, but still the wind took him." The medicine man, Owl Feather, wore a worried frown.

"Lame Deer went to the sacred mountain to pray for peace," the chief said. "The people have rebelled against Spanish rule for many years and never met with any success. But now the Pueblos are united, and seven suns ago we received a deerskin with the message that the Northern Pueblos are planning a revolt against the Spaniards. They are urging that all the Pueblos join."

"And we should," Owl Feather said. "The Spaniards are evil and greedy men. They are not friends of the Tewa people."

"You and I have always been friends, Chief Leaping Antelope," Father said. "And I have many friends among the other Indians as well."

"That is true, yet I am worried. It makes no difference if a Spaniard is good or evil, all are in danger. Father Marcos did not come to the pueblo as planned. Where is he? He is a reliable man and very honorable, but he did not come."

"Do you think he has been harmed in some way?"

"I don't know, but you should post guards. And take your sheep and cattle to the mountains or canyons to keep them safe. I will inform you when the war starts."

Father frowned. "Do you have any idea how long before the war will start?"

"I can't say for sure. A messenger will come to us bearing a knotted cord. Each knot will tell us the number of sunsets until we attack. But the warriors are restless. I don't know how much longer the elders can hold them back."

Father turned to me. "I need to stay at the hacienda to prepare in the event unfriendly Indians come to the ranch. Ride up to the sheep camps in the morning, Diego, and send the flocks into the canyon, even though it is early in the season for winter pasture."

"I'll ride with you, Diego," White Wolf said.

I nodded my thanks, but all through the rest of the evening, a worry I couldn't name pestered me.

CHAPTER 6
Estrella's Journal

Tonight, I am confused and feel strange. While Pedro told us the story, I watched White Wolf. My heart thumped and my stomach churned. He sat cross-legged, with his wrists resting on his knees, hands hanging limp. After Pedro finished the story, I asked White Wolf to come with me to the millpond.

We sat on a log and for a few minutes watched the dragonflies dart about. "Why did you want to see me, Estrella?" White Wolf asked.

"I want to paint your picture, just the way you sat while Pedro told us the story."

He sat on the ground. I sat facing him, our knees touching. "Like this?" he grinned.

He is so beautiful a lump caught in my throat, and I could scarcely breathe. He smelled of wind and sunshine and something I couldn't name. I leaned toward him and with trembling fingers reached out and traced the line of his jaw, the plane of his cheeks, the curve of his lips.

White Wolf clutched my wrist and looked deep into my eyes. "What game are you playing, Estrella?" he asked.

"No game." I stared back without blinking.

He rose to his feet and pulled me with him. "Come," he said. "They are waiting for us. I will give this some thought."

He held my wrist while we walked to the house. My brain swirled in confusion. I peeked at White Wolf from under my eyelashes. He was like a rock beside me, but I felt the heat of his body and a strange warmth spread through me. For some reason I could not eat my dinner.

The candle is burning low, so I must go to bed. There is a full moon tonight, but very little light shows through the mica covered window. Still—I don't know that I will sleep...

I didn't sleep much last night and in the dim light of morning dressed quietly so as not to disturb Marta. Old as I am, she still sleeps in my bedroom. My bed is on an adobe bench with a fireplace built into it that helps keep me warm in winter. Marta's bed does not have a fireplace.

I didn't bother to braid my hair. I pulled open the door and stepped outside, the sun was but a hint on the eastern horizon.

I started for the chicken coop and caught my breath when I saw White Wolf. With arms outstretched and head thrown back, he gazed at the coral streak in the sky. I knew he was saying his morning prayers, and my conscience twitched because I'd forgotten to say my own prayers.

White Wolf wore no shirt; his fingers were flecked with white from his cornmeal offering. The first rays of the sun gleamed like gold on his finely molded muscles and picked out the turquoise stone on the leather thong he wore around his neck. He looked like the drawing of one of the statues in Diego's Greek book, and my heart hammered so hard I thought it would leap out of my chest.

I said a quick Ave Maria, combed my hair with my fingers, pinched my cheeks to make them rosy, and smoothed my skirt. He turned when he heard my footstep on the pebble path. He didn't say a word, but his dark eyes kindled with pleasure when he saw me.

I told him that I needed a new quill and planned to get a tail feather from the white goose before she woke up, and he said he'd help me.

We walked to the hen yard in silence. The goose slept with her head tucked under a wing. White Wolf plucked a feather, and she looked up with a surprised honk. The old black rooster awoke, flapped his wings, flew to the top of a corral post, and announced morning with a raucous squawk. We both laughed, and with a grin, White Wolf handed me the feather.

I thanked him, then suddenly shy, lowered my eyes. This bothered me. I've known White Wolf all my life; there is no reason to be shy around him.

He asked if I wanted him to sharpen the feather for me. I glanced at the big knife on his belt, shook my head and smiled. It takes a delicate touch and a small penknife to sharpen the nib of a quill.

He said that he was leaving for the sheep camps with Diego in an hour, and I told him I knew that. Then he said that we'd talk when he returned. I nodded. I want to see him, I want to talk to him, I want to touch him, and that makes me feel strange, but happy. I don't understand *what's happening to me.*

White Wolf gazed into my eyes for a moment. With two fingers he lifted a strand of my hair. "It shines like copper," he said in a low voice. He brushed my cheek with the tips of his fingers and said that my skin was soft and smooth as the petals of a yucca blossom. Then he smiled and said, "You are pleasant to look at, Rainbow."

Before I could answer, he turned and walked toward the river. I watched until he was out of sight...

CHAPTER 7

OUR HOUSE WAS made of adobe bricks plastered with clay; the interior walls were whitewashed with gypsum. In the kitchen, Estrella had painted a border of yellow flowers near the ceiling. Healing and cooking herbs hung from the rafters. An adobe bench ran along the wall on each side of the fireplace. Wooden shelves held pewter and clay dishes. Alcoves built into the walls held baskets, clay pots, and wooden trenchers.

We sat at the kitchen table to eat breakfast. While Father gave thanks for the bounty, a swallow flew in through the barred window, snatched a fly and darted out. Marta filled our pewter plates with a corn and bean stew. We had goat cheese smothered in sorghum molasses for dessert.

"Ride El Cid, Diego." Father said as he walked with White Wolf and me to the corrals. I looked at him in astonishment. Only Father ever touched his gray horse.

"I've trained him well for battle, and you may come across unfriendly Indians," Father said. "Perhaps you should leave your spurs home. He obeys the slightest touch and will come when you whistle."

I knew the whistle. I'd often heard Father call his horse and delighted at the sight of El Cid, silver mane and tail flying, galloping to Father. "Let the horse get to know you," he said.

I stroked El Cid's velvet muzzle and talked in a quiet voice. He blew through his nose and snuffled my neck. I caught the fresh scent of green grass and horse. I rubbed his chest and ran my hands down his legs and under his belly, talking all the while. I don't know what words I used, but El Cid seemed to like it. I went to the stable to get my saddle and the horse followed. Esteban gave me a different saddle, one of the new ones that had the saddlebags attached. I threw the saddle over the horse's back and pulled the single cinch tight. I coiled my rawhide rope over the saddle horn.

I strapped my sword around my waist, shoved a long-bladed knife in my belt, and tucked my small knife inside my boot. We went to the courtyard and White Wolf and I drew water from the well, filled our leather water bags, and hung them from the saddle horns.

White Wolf and all the Indians from his pueblo used saddles Saul Guzman made for them. Their horses were a gift from Father, and although most of the Pueblo Indians do not often ride horses, the Cucuri are excellent horsemen. I tried to hide the nagging worry I carried in the back of my mind, and we rode from the hacienda in high spirits.

We headed our horses northwest to the high summer

pastures where the shepherd, Juan, tended the larger herd.

A band of wild horses grazed on a hillside. A black stallion switched his tail and stomped his foot, and with a wary eye watched us ride past his herd.

I said, "Sometimes it bothers me that the Apache steal our ranch horses when there are these for the taking. When we need horses, we capture a few wild ones. They could do the same."

"Yes," White Wolf said, "but why should they when you do it for them and besides stealing saves them time."

"These mustangs are not difficult to capture, and it doesn't take long to train them."

White Wolf shook his head. "The Apache like the way your vaqueros train a horse."

"We'd teach them our way; they wouldn't need to steal." I realized that I resented the thievery and loss of livestock that had become an accustomed way of life and determined to talk with Father once again about it.

The sun was low in the west before we reached the farthest sheep camp tucked in a high mountain meadow. Hundreds of the four-horned sheep covered the hillside. Mixed with the sheep were goats, many of them black—one black goat for every one hundred head of sheep. Surprised to see us, Juan, the shepherd, greeted us with a broad grin that showed two missing teeth.

I told him about the Indians starting a war and that the canyon was the safest place for the sheep so they wouldn't be stolen or slaughtered. "Start the sheep to the canyon first thing in the morning, Juan. Hurry them along, you don't have much time."

"It is too early in the season for winter pasture, Diego.

I have my sling and my dogs. I can protect the sheep."

"No, Juan. Don Rafael sent me to tell you to move the sheep. You are to meet Lopé in the canyon and combine the flocks. That way you won't be alone in case of trouble."

Juan nodded. He would not argue with my father's orders.

White Wolf and I spent the night at the sheep camp. I lay wrapped in my blanket watching the stars and thinking about the war until I fell asleep.

Early the next morning, Juan placed two fingers in his mouth and whistled. The dogs ran out from under a bush and Juan made a circular motion with his arm. The dogs rounded up the sheep and goats. Juan pointed to the southwest and the lead goat, wearing a tinkling bell, started the sheep on their slow trek to the canyon. The sheep bleated and danced about. The agile dogs nipped at the hindquarters of any stray and kept the sheep in line.

Juan dismantled and packed his camp on his burro. With a wave of his hand, he followed the herd. White Wolf and I watched until the flock disappeared over the hill, then we turned our horses eastward.

We reached the other sheep camp at mid-day. Lopé, the shepherd, was not an old man, but his face was weathered with creases around his eyes from long hours of squinting in the bright sun. I gave him his orders and he headed his flock to the canyon without any argument.

White Wolf and I turned our horses toward home. We hadn't gone many leagues when we heard a low rumbling in the distance. A dusty haze hung on the eastern horizon and the wind carried the stench of buffalo toward us. We rode until our path was blocked by the enormous herd that stretched eastward for many leagues.

Buffalo covered the prairie as far as the eye could see. The huge creatures were tall as a horse, larger than a fighting bull. A mass of wool covered the buffaloes' shoulders and hung past the knees. The hump on their backs was like that of a camel. Great clumps of fleece hung down their massive heads ending in a woolly beard. Their short tails had a tuft of hair on the end. Calves bleated, calling for their mothers. Cows lowed in answer. Bulls grunted and snorted as they pushed one another with their curved horns and stabbed at the earth with their sharp hooves.

Wolves darted through the herd waiting for a downed buffalo or lost calf. Birds rode on the buffaloes' backs pecking at fleas and lice. Although we didn't see any, neither White Wolf nor I had any doubt that hunters rode the fringes picking off stragglers.

We chose a young bull that was ambling on the edge of the herd. Buffalo would stampede at sight of a tumbleweed so I inched El Cid close to the bull. In one swift motion I drove my sword into the bull's neck, between the hump and the skull. He stopped, head down and, splay legged, swayed. White Wolf stabbed the buffalo in the ribs with his lance and the bull went down on his knees. I pulled my sword from his neck, thrust it into his side and the buffalo toppled over. He gave three powerful kicks and lay still. I jumped from my horse and quickly slashed the bull's throat. The herd moved away from the downed buffalo and plodded on their southward journey.

Several wolves sat on their haunches, pink tongues lolling out the sides of their mouths and watched as we butchered the buffalo. We slit the belly open and tossed the contents to the wolves. Snarling and yelping, they devoured the meat and sat, watching, waiting for more.

White Wolf and I camped for the night in the shadow of the blue mesa, listening to the vast buffalo herd rumble past. As I sat by the campfire, I thought about Lame Deer and wondered what happened to him up on the mesa so that he had never returned.

Early the next morning only a few straggling buffalo dotted the plains. We packed what meat we could carry and left the remainder for the wolves. As we headed south to my father's ranch, I still carried an unnamed worry in the back of my mind, so I was eager to get home.

"Do you know why the Pueblos are trying to overthrow the Spanish government?" I asked White Wolf.

"The Tewa Pueblos have been under Spanish rule for many years," he said. "And the Spaniards have been very cruel. They have made slaves of our people and destroyed our gods. They moved into our homes and lived in our pueblos as though they owned them so that many of us have no shelter from the wind and rain. They have stolen our corn and left us to starve through the harsh winters. Children have been snatched from their parents and sent to Mexico as slaves. Those of us who rebelled have been beaten and carry the whip scars on our backs, others have had their hands and feet chopped off. Many died from these and other tortures, leaving women and children with no man to protect them. Now a strong and brave man from the Taos Pueblo is leading us out of slavery and we are answering the call."

"It's coming soon, Diego," he said, "and I hear that even though they are the sworn enemy of the Pueblos, the Navajo and the Apache are joining the revolt. If that happens, no Spaniard will be safe in the Tewa Nation. You must urge your father to take his family and flee."

A cold shiver ran down my spine, and I felt a strange need to hurry home. I nudged El Cid to a trot.

White Wolf caught up with me. "I will help your family escape, Diego. I will fight beside you." I didn't answer; there was no need. Long ago we had pledged our lifelong friendship.

When we were young boys, we had ridden to a sacred mountain in a quest for our visions. We had painted our bodies with yellow lightning bolts and red and black symbols, and then we fasted for twenty-four hours. When we awoke from our sleep, I had not seen my vision, but listened in awe as White Wolf told me his. He had seen himself riding a black horse across the sky. He carried a blue bundle in his arms and rode under rainbows of brilliant hues. The horse would touch the ground for a moment, then race across the sky to another rainbow. That day on the mountain, we discussed the vision for many hours, but neither of us could work out the meaning of the dream. Then we each made a cut on our wrists, and in our secret handshake clasped one another by the right wrist and, as our blood mingled, pledged undying loyalty. Although we both bear the scars on our wrists, from that day on, we neither one spoke of the vision again.

I now knew the name of my worry: The Pueblo Rebellion. It crowded all other thoughts from my mind, and we rode in silence. Clouds heavy with rain formed in the west. Thunder rumbled and jagged forks of lightning pierced the leaden sky. The crops would welcome the rain, and maybe it would slow the Indian revolt.

CHAPTER 8
Estrella's Journal

I knew I should not have gone riding alone this afternoon. But I was restless and bored and tired of women's work. I'd spent the morning grinding corn, weeding the garden, dying wool, and then Marta wanted me to card and spin the wool. But Mama said I could have a few minutes to myself.

I ran to the stable. No one was around, so I saddled my little bay mare, Bonita. Both Mama and Papa have warned me many times to never ride far from the hacienda, and never alone. It is too dangerous. But I am not afraid. The Pueblo Indians are our friends and the Apache and Navajo live far away. But I had not intended to ride very far.

I rode downstream. The river, swollen from the downpour in the mountains, rippled and ran hard and fast. The waves splashed against the banks and murmured a happy tune.

I breathed in the hot smell of summer and rode Bonita

at a slow walk beneath the cool shade of the dusty cottonwood trees, enjoying my freedom and thinking about a name for the new puppy. A noise startled me, and I looked around. I saw nothing and decided it was my imagination, or a rabbit scurrying through the brush.

Bright red and yellow flowers across the river caught my eye. Here, the gravel bar gave the horse firm footing. It seemed a safe place to cross and I urged Bonita down the slippery bank and into the river. She waded into the water with dainty steps and paused to drink. I leaned forward and stroked her glossy neck, called her pretty names and pressed her on. She snorted, shook her head, and sprinkled me with water. I laughed and slapped her rump with my leather riding crop.

Bonita lunged and without warning she was swimming. A wave washed over me. I couldn't stay in the saddle. The water was over my head. I don't know how to swim. I couldn't breathe. My chest felt as though a heavy hand held me down. With eyes shut tight, I flailed my arms. My head broke the surface. I coughed and spit water. Another wave splashed over me. I was under water again. I flapped my arms. I touched something hard and slick—the saddle! I clutched at it, but couldn't hold on.

Somewhere in the back of my head, I heard the vaqueros talking, "If you ever lose your seat in a river, grab your horse's tail, he'll pull you out." Keep calm, I told myself, Bonita is here. I grasped her tail and the blessed horse kept swimming. Suddenly my feet touched ground and I opened my eyes. We were on the far shore. Bonita shook herself like a dog and scrambled up the steep slope.

I pushed my dripping hair from my face and crawled up the bank. I heard laughter, and there Black Bear stood with an ugly grin crinkling his face. I was angry in an instant. Although he hasn't visited the rancho much in the last few years, I've known Black Bear all my life.

"Black Bear, I almost drowned and you stood here on shore laughing. You didn't even try to save me."

"You didn't seem to need any help. You swim pretty good and did all right without me."

"What do you mean? I was in that river for the longest time trying to get out. Another minute and I would have drowned for sure."

Black Bear snickered. "You were in the water for maybe one minute, that's all."

I couldn't believe it. If that was true it was the longest minute of my life. "Even so, I could have drowned."

"In those wet clothes, maybe," he leered.

I looked down. My muddy skirt clung to my legs, my blouse hugged my breasts, and my shawl hung limp down my back. I tied the shawl across my chest, pulled the skirt from my legs and shook it out.

I was irritated. I was soaking wet, covered in mud, Black Bear was laughing at me, my horse grazed as though we hadn't been through the most terrifying moment of my life, and I had to cross the river again to get home.

Then something Black Bear said struck me. He said that I was a good swimmer. I'd never even been in the river before and I swam! I stood on the bank and watched the waves crash against rocks. Now the river's song sounded threatening and sinister.

"I can show you a place where you can cross without getting wet," Black Bear said.

"Even when the river is this high?"

"Yes, it's wider than here, but shallow."

"Thank you then, I'd appreciate it."

He chuckled again. I had no idea what he found so funny, but he helped me mount Bonita and we headed down river.

About half an hour later we came to the shallow crossing. I looked at it with apprehension.

Black Bear smirked. "Are you afraid?"

I shook my head and set my jaw. No matter what, I would not have Black Bear laugh at me again, but I'd hoped he would offer to ride across with me. I urged Bonita into the water and clutched her mane with both hands. She crossed the river with no difficulty.

I turned to wave at Black Bear, but he turned his back and loped away.

Bonita trotted toward home. It was a long way, and I had time to think about what I would tell Papa about riding so far alone...

No one was in the corrals when I got home from the dunking in the river. I unsaddled Bonita and ran to my little bedroom. I washed my face and changed clothes and went to the kitchen. Mama and Marta had packed food, clothing, and medicinal herbs in bundles.

"Where are you taking those things?" I asked Mama.

"We were looking for you, Estrella. Where have you been? We are taking these to the guard tower; we'll be staying there for a few days. From his lookout, Pedro spied some hostile Indians. They shot at him, but Gracias a Dios the arrow missed. Come help."

I grabbed a bundle, and Mama and I crossed the courtyard and away from the house to the guard tower where we all crowded into the lower level. The men gain the upper level through an opening in the ceiling and a *ladder. The tower is made of stone and is used to store grain and weapons. Several clay jars of water stood in a corner. Someone had brought in wood and built a cooking fire in the fireplace. The heat and crowded room made the air heavy and breathing difficult.*

I climbed the ladder to the upper level. Men were stationed at the window slits armed with muskets and bows. A small cannon was pointed through one of the windows. I peeked through one of the slits. Indians on horseback milled about on the pasture outside the gate.

"What are they doing here, Papa?"

"They probably came for horses, but I sent Clemente and Manuel with most of the herd to the canyons. The others are in the courtyard."

I thought about Bonita stabled at the corrals, but didn't say anything. Maybe the Indians wouldn't find her.

"You should not be here, Estrella," Papa said. "Go down with the women. The Apache may attack at any time."

I climbed back down the ladder and talked with Rebecca. I told her what had happened to me at the river.

"You must have been terribly frightened, Estrella. But I thought you weren't allowed to ride alone."

"I'm not, but I didn't intend to ride so far. And now poor Bonita is in the stable all alone. Maybe I can sneak her into the courtyard before the Apache find her."

"Don't try it, Estrella. Your father would not like it, and you might get hurt."

We found a place near the door. We wrapped ourselves in blankets and lay down for the night. I didn't sleep. All night I fretted. I worried about Bonita and I worried that Diego would come home and the Indians would ambush him.

Olivia Godat

This morning the rains started. I climbed back up the ladder to check on the Indians. They'd camped under trees and built fires. Papa sent me back down the ladder.

Now I am sitting on my bedroll and leaning against the door writing in my journal. I hear the puppy whimpering and scratching at the door. I want to let him in but I know that no one else wants the odor of a wet dog in these cramped quarters. I can't leave the poor little thing out in the rain, he doesn't even have a name yet. The Apache seemed quiet enough; it looked as though they were eating breakfast. I'll sneak out and put the puppy in the storeroom.

I don't want anyone to read my journal, so I'll hide it in my blankets, then when no one is looking, I'll slip out the door...

CHAPTER 9
Diego

LATER, WHEN WE were on the Blue Mesa, I learned how Black Bear had kidnapped Estrella.

My sister had stacked her bedroll against the door and listened to the puppy whine. The whimpering changed to a high-pitched squeal followed by yelps and loud shrieks. Then silence.

Estrella slipped out the door. The rain beat down in a constant frenzy. She pulled her shawl over her head and peered through the heavy rain. "Here, puppy, puppy. Where are you?" Estrella wished she'd found a suitable name for the little dog. He was so sweet, she'd wanted to call him *Dulce*, but that was the name of Rebecca's horse. Estrella dashed across the empty space to the courtyard calling for the puppy.

A strong arm grasped her around the waist and a heavy hand pressed against her mouth. "I found your puppy," said a harsh voice.

Estrella kicked and squirmed. She reached up to scratch her captor's face. She bit down on the rough hand and tasted blood. She clamped her teeth tighter and shook her head like a dog shaking a rat.

"No use fighting, I'm stronger than you," said the voice. He moved his hand from her mouth and slammed her face down to the ground. She twisted her body to see whom she was fighting and he placed a knee on her stomach.

"Black Bear! What do you want?"

"There's your puppy." Black Bear gestured toward a small shape lying in the mud with an arrow in its side. "I knew you'd come out when you heard it squealing."

"What did you do to it? You didn't have to kill it; he was just a small puppy," Estrella said. "How could you do such a thing?"

"I did your family a favor," he sneered. "He's fat and tender and will make a nice meal. They'll thank me when they run out of food. Enough talk, you're coming with me." Black Bear pulled her to her feet.

"I won't go with you. What do you want? Let me go. I'll call my father."

"No need for you to shout. No one can hear you over the rain. By the way, I like you in wet clothes," he leered and pulled her by the arm.

"I'm not going anywhere with you. Let me go." Estrella kicked him in the shins. The deluge turned into a drizzle. "Help, help," she shouted, and butted him in the stomach.

"You want to give me trouble? I'll show you what trouble is." Black Bear slapped her. Her head reeled. He gritted his teeth and tied her wrists with a length of horsehair rope. He snatched off his dirty, blue headband

and gagged her. Estrella continued to struggle.

"At least I don't have to listen to your squawking now." He dragged her behind him. Estrella pulled back and fell. "You're going with me," he said. "You can't get away." He tied her ankles with a leather thong and carried her over his shoulder to the corral. "Thank you for keeping your horse in the corral." Black Bear threw her face down over Bonita's back. He climbed on his own horse and led Bonita away from the ranch at a lope. With every stride Estrella bounced and tried to roll off the horse.

Black Bear held her on with one hand, then finally reined to a stop beside a large rock formation. With his knife, he cut the leather bindings from her ankles. "We have a long way to go. If you fall off the horse it will only slow me down, so hang on or I'll tie you on." Black Bear set Estrella astride the horse.

She mumbled into the gag. "I won't take that off," said Black Bear. "You talk so much that it hurts my ears."

He led Bonita in widening circles until a group of Apache warriors joined them. Joking and laughing they rode their ponies over Bonita's hoof-prints until her tracks were no longer clear.

Then the warriors separated, one group rode south, the other continued north.

The sun was low when they arrived at a small village of huts made of slender poles covered with brush and grass. Black Bear led Estrella to an empty wickiup that smelled of sheep and old grease. A stained sheepskin lay on the dirt floor, tightly woven baskets sat around the ashes of a cold fire. He shoved her onto the sheepskin, bound her ankles, and removed the gag.

"Where am I and what are you going to do with me?"

Estrella asked.

"You're in the village of my people, and it won't do any good to scream and yell. No one will come to help you. You are my captive."

"What do you want of me? My father will find you."

"I don't think so," Black Bear said with a smirk. "Your father is too busy fighting off an attack of Apache warriors."

"Why are you doing this, Black Bear? I thought we were friends."

"No Spaniard is a friend of mine. But don't worry, I won't harm you. It's your brother I want."

"What did Diego ever do to you?"

Black Bear shrugged. "He's a Spaniard, proud, like you, and everyone thinks he is brave and daring. He'll come looking for you, Estrella, and when he does—we'll see just how brave he is."

"Don't hurt him, Black Bear, I beg you. Please don't hurt him."

Black Bear gave an evil laugh. "I've had enough of this talk." He turned to leave then said, "I planned to bring you here when we met at the river, but my people wanted to know more about your father's defense and weapons. That's why they attacked your ranch. Now we know about the muskets and the skill of your people with the bow." He eyed her with admiration. "You are brave, Estrella. You'd be a worthy wife for an Apache, if you didn't talk so much, and, if you weren't Spanish."

Estrella kicked at him with her bound feet, her eyes flashed. "I hope Diego kills you."

"I go now to find him and then we'll see which of us gets killed." Black Bear left the wickiup chuckling.

CHAPTER 10

THE AIR WAS filled with the smell of rain. Sudden fat drops pelted the ground and sent bits of dust flying. Soon the rain beat down in a torrent, but I wouldn't stop. The worry of the rebellion spurred me on.

White Wolf rode through the downpour beside me. We covered our heads with our woolen ponchos and sat hunched in the saddle against the beating rain. Water ran in sheets across the thirsty plains and our horses slogged through the mud with their heads down.

The rain gradually eased, and by the time we were less than an hour from the ranch, it turned to a drizzle. The sun shone weakly through a watery haze, and in a short time the rain stopped. We wrung the water out of our blankets the best we could and draped them across our horses' rumps to dry.

Neither White Wolf nor I said a word during our ride to the ranch. The hacienda lay over the next rise. I reined in El Cid and listened. We heard shouting and the sound of horses running. "I think we should go around the hill and approach from the river side."

"It sounds as though they are under attack."

"Maybe, I don't know, White Wolf. Something is wrong and I don't want to take chances." We heard the roar of a musket and glanced at one another in alarm.

We turned our horses to the north and rode around the hill, through a slight depression by the river, and to the fields and orchard. The rain had smashed the corn and wheat into the mud. Unripe peaches lay on the ground. I didn't stop to assess any further damage.

No one was at the house. Horses milled about in the courtyard. I jumped off El Cid and ran to the guard tower. My boots slipped in the mud and my wet buckskin clothes stuck to my body, cold and slimy. I pounded on the heavy wooden door of the guardhouse. "It's me, Diego. Let me in."

The door creaked open and Rebecca peeked out. "Diego, come in. The Apache attacked us."

I slipped inside with White Wolf right behind me. I heard the blast of my father's musket. Then Gaspar's. I climbed the ladder and peered out the window. The Apache stood in a group, too far for us to be effective with either the bow or the musket. Arrows lay scattered about on the green expanse between us. "Is anybody hurt?" I asked Father.

"No, they haven't come near. They stand just out of range. They don't seem to be interested in fighting and want only to harass us. We've shot a few cannon balls at them, but I want to save our powder."

"How long has this lasted?" I asked.

"This is the second day. They came yesterday and shot a few arrows. They camped the night over in those trees and stayed there during the rainstorm. They're out again now but are just shouting taunts and backing off. Some have already left."

Relieved, I said, "Maybe they just want to remind us they are our enemies. Maybe this is not yet the start of the Rebellion."

"There's Leaping Antelope," White Wolf said. "Now all the Apache are leaving."

Chief Leaping Antelope led his people down the hill toward the house. One by one the Apache slipped into the trees without shooting an arrow.

"The danger is over," Father said. "We can go back to our houses." All the men climbed down the ladder.

In the crowded lower level, Rebecca tugged at my sleeve, and I was suddenly aware of my wet and blood splattered clothes. "Diego," she whispered, "I don't know where Estrella is. I can't find her anywhere."

"Did she come into the tower?"

"Yes, she was here this morning during the rain. But I haven't seen her for a couple of hours."

"Maybe she went to the house for something."

"Her blankets and journal are still here."

"Have you talked to Mother or Marta about this?"

"No. Diego, but I'm really worried. She wanted to sneak out last night and take care of Bonita. I talked her out of that. This morning she was fretting about the puppy."

My stomach dropped and my mouth went dry. "I'll go to the house and see if she's there." I headed for the door.

White Wolf was by my side. "What is it?"

"Estrella has disappeared."

"I will find her," White Wolf said in a grim voice. I looked at him in astonishment, his jaw was taut, his eyes slits of obsidian ice.

"Bring the journal," I told Rebecca. "Maybe there's something in it that will tell us where she went."

"You mustn't read her journal," she said.

"I will read it." I walked out the door, White Wolf behind me. Rebecca followed with the journal.

The parched earth had soaked up the rain puddles, and I strode through the milling horses. Behind a clay oven, I found the puppy's body pinned to the ground with an arrow. White Wolf examined the arrow. "Black Bear's," he said.

I didn't question him. I knew White Wolf recognized the arrow, but I didn't want to believe that Black Bear would harm my sister. The sun glinted off a shiny object. I picked up Estrella's sapphire pendant and showed it to White Wolf.

"The mud shows signs of a struggle. Black Bear has her." He spoke with such certainty that I knew it to be true.

"See if you can find tracks. If not, I'll follow the Apache warriors," I said and handed Rebecca the broken necklace. "Take care of this and her journal, please. I'm going to tell my parents, and then I'll go after Estrella. I'll find her and I'll bring her back."

White Wolf took the necklace from Rebecca. "I'll take care of this."

I raised my eyebrows in question.

"We may need it," is all he said and strode off.

In the crowded guardroom, my father stood among a knot of people with his arm around my mother. I didn't know how to tell them about my sister, so I blurted out, "We think Black Bear has kidnapped Estrella." I heard a gasp and couldn't bear to look at my mother. I closed my ears to Marta's lamentations.

Father's face had gone ashen. "Why do you say that?"

I told him what White Wolf and I found. "I'm leaving now to find her. White Wolf is searching for tracks."

I saw the conflicting emotions on my father's face. "I should go with you, Diego, but I must stay and protect our people." His shoulders sagged and he said, "Do everything you can to bring our little Star home safe."

Mother moved from his side. "Change into dry clothes, Diego, you are drenched from the rain. Gaspar, ready his weapons. See to his horse, Esteban." Mother seldom issues orders, but when she does, everyone obeys in an instant and without question.

"Come, Marta," she said, "we must see to Diego's clothes and prepare food for him to take."

"I don't need fresh clothes, Mother."

"You don't know where you're going or how long you'll be gone, Diego. You can't take the chance of becoming ill in those wet clothes."

I didn't argue, and by the time I'd changed to dry buckskin trousers, a cotton shirt, buckskin jacket, and dry boots, El Cid was saddled and Esteban had rubbed him free of mud. "I'll come with you, Diego, I'm ready now."

I pulled on my knee-length leather chaps. "No, Esteban, you're needed here to care for the livestock."

Esteban nodded with that look he sometimes gave me, as though measuring my worth, and slung two leather water flasks over the saddle horn.

Gaspar tied a rolled blanket to the back of the saddle.

"My musket is in there, Don Diego." I blinked at the title as he handed me a powder horn and a leather bag of musket balls. He had cleaned and shined my sword and placed it in the scabbard tied to the saddle. I shoved my large knife in my belt and made sure my boot knife was in its sheath.

I shook his hand. "Take care of the ranch, Gaspar."

"With my life, *Señor*." I shook my head in confusion. When had the change from *Chico* to *Señor* taken place?

Mother came out with a packet of food. I bent and kissed her forehead goodbye. She reached up, placed her arms around my neck and kissed my cheek. "*Vaya con Dios*, my son. Go with God."

I tightened the chinstraps of my hat and with a wave trotted out of the courtyard.

White Wolf met me at the gate. "Did you find any tracks?" I asked.

He nodded, "They point north and he is leading Bonita."

I extended my hand. "Thanks for your help, my friend."

"I'm going with you."

"There's no need."

"Yes," he said, "there is. I must find Estrella."

I saw the set look on his face and knew I couldn't change his mind. I nodded. "Let's go then." In truth, I was glad for his company. I knew now that Black Bear was my enemy and White Wolf knew him better than I did. I needed all the help I could get.

White Wolf had no water flask so I handed him one of mine. "We'll share the water and food." He took the water without comment and hung it on his saddle horn.

We rode in silence for about three leagues following the tracks of two ponies. Bonita wore horseshoes so her prints were clear. The rain had washed the dust from the grass and brush. Everything looked bright and clean. The sun dipped behind the mountains, daylight faded and the tracks became mixed with many others.

"It is too dark to tell if these tracks are Indian ponies or wild horses."

"We'll find a good place and make camp for the night."

"No," White Wolf said, "I'll go on. I know where the Apache live."

His determination amazed me. "He may have broken away from the group and taken Estrella elsewhere."

"Yes," White Wolf agreed. "His tribe doesn't live north, but they may have moved their village."

"If they have moved their village, you won't know where to go and it's too dark now to track them. You might miss the trail, or worse yet, cover their tracks with your own."

White Wolf stared at the deepening night. Finally, he nodded. "You're right, Diego. It is best we wait for daylight." But I could tell he was not happy about the enforced wait.

We made dry camp in a piñon tree grove near a rock wall that cast long shadows in the moonlight. We shared a meager meal of dried meat and sips of water. I wrapped myself in my blanket, and the last thing I remember before sleep claimed me was the singing coyotes and White Wolf studying the stars.

I woke before sunup and saw White Wolf sitting on his heels gazing at the dawn. "Did you sleep?" I asked.

"Enough. Are you ready?"

I nodded and noticed the saddled horses. White Wolf would push hard today. That suited me, and we chewed on jerky while we followed the tracks north. The sun was three hours old when White Wolf said, "There is Bonita's hoof print."

We traveled in silence for another hour, my mind full of worry for my sister. I glanced at White Wolf. With his mouth set in a grim line he leaned from the saddle; his eyes never wavered from the track.

At last he spoke, "The tracks have separated." He reined his horse to a stop and dismounted. I jumped from El Cid. We squatted and studied the tracks in the dried dirt. One group turned southeast, the other northwest. We could no longer determine which print belonged to Bonita. The other horses had blotted them out.

"They're going in opposite directions, which will we follow?"

"We too, will separate," White Wolf said. "You go west and I'll head south. That's where Black Bear's people live."

"Estrella is my sister. If you think that is where they have her, I should be the one to face the Apache."

White Wolf looked at me, his eyes hard and determined. "I will be the one to bring Rainbow to safety." He swung onto his horse and galloped away to the south, leaving me to stare after him.

I mounted El Cid and followed the tracks leading westward.

The trail led me around mesas and red sandstone towers. At times I lost the track in the rock covered ground. Then I'd find where the track doubled back and it took me in another direction, then it turned to the west again, and I knew that Black Bear enjoyed this game he played. I could feel eyes on me and scanned the rocks for a glimpse of my enemy but saw nothing.

I rode into a thick stand of piñon and juniper and dismounted. I would wait here for Black Bear. My water flask still held a small amount, so I poured the water into my hat and gave it to El Cid. He drank it all and licked my hat to get the last drops. I stroked my brave horse and apologized. I promised we'd find water soon. I sucked on a pebble to relieve my own thirst.

An hour passed with no movement. In the sky, an eagle floated on air currents. Near my foot, a lizard skittered under a rock. A sparrow fluttered in the piñon branches. Heat waves shimmered on the distant blue mesa. Insects hummed. I watched a spider spin its web between two trees. I caught the scent of my horse's sweat. The sun was high and my patience was low.

I led El Cid through the forest and looked for greenery that indicated nearby water. Near a stone outcropping, I saw dampness around a bush that hinted water was close by. I scouted around and found a small spring seeping through a crevice in the rocks. I used my large knife as a pick. With a flat rock for a scoop, I made a wide depression in the ground and lined it with stones. The trickle dribbled into the crude basin until there was enough water for El Cid. After he drank, I filled my water bag and hung it on the saddle.

I bent to dip my hand in the water and a shadow flickered across the rocks. I turned. Pain exploded in my head. Colored lights blurred my vision. I tumbled into a dark abyss and blackness.

CHAPTER 11
Diego's Vision

I BECAME AWARE of a pinpoint of light in the blackness and the faint sounds of battle: swords clashing, men's hoarse shouts. The dim light glowed brighter and brighter until the darkness was clear as the morning sky and the battle sounds had grown loud and fierce.

I was on a hillside overlooking a green valley. A horde of Apache Indians outnumbered a small squadron of armor-clad conquistadors. The Apache surrounded them and many a brave conquistador lay wounded on the field. I touched El Cid in the flanks with my heels and we galloped down the hill. I pulled out my sword and slashed about with the blade. I shouted, "Santiago y Montez" and entered the fray. Others took up the battle cry to the soldier-saint and fought with renewed vigor.

El Cid jumped over my fallen comrades, and I pinned a warrior with my lance. I deflected arrows with my shield, and again called on my patron saint.

A white charger with a gold saddle appeared at my side, on his back a man in a gold suit and glistening white cloak. With his golden sword the man fought beside me and together we cut the enemy down as though they were stalks of ripe wheat. The Apache scattered like the winnowed grain.

I brandished my sword and shouted, "For Santiago and the glory of Spain." The man smiled, made a sign with his hand and blessed me. In awe, I stared as a white cloud descended and gathered up the man and his horse.

I knelt and reached out my hand. "Santiago."

"Rescue your family," he said. The golden plume in his white hat fluttered and he disappeared into the clouds.

Again darkness. My head throbbed. "Santiago," I mumbled.

CHAPTER 12
Black Bear's Wickiup

"DIEGO, DIEGO. ARE you awake?"

Estrella's voice. I opened my eyes and attempted to focus through the fog. I tried to answer but only groaned. I wanted to sit up but couldn't move. My hands were tied behind my back.

"You're tied up, Diego. We both are bound hand and foot. I can't get loose. Lie still, you're hurt."

"Water," I croaked.

"I'll try, just a minute. My hands are tied in front, and I'm able to get my own drink of water, so maybe..."

I heard shuffling and scraping on the ground.

Minutes passed before I heard Estrella speak, "Here, drink this."

A gourd dipper pressed against my face. I opened my dry lips and tepid water spilled on my chin and dribbled down my parched throat. "Where are we? How did I get here?" The last thing I remembered was my vision of the battle with the Apache.

"Black Bear's wickiup. He brought you here last evening. I was so worried, Diego, you've been unconscious for the longest time."

"I can't tell, is it day or night? It hurts to open my eyes."

"Keep them closed then. Black Bear is waiting for you to wake up, and then he has something planned for you. I don't know what, but I'm sure it's nothing pleasant. The longer you can lie still, the stronger you'll be."

I didn't want to move. I wanted to go back to sleep. "What time is it?"

"Late afternoon. Hush, I hear someone coming."

I heard Black Bear's harsh voice. "Is he awake?"

"No, he's not and I'm worried." Estrella did sound worried. "Cut the ropes around my wrists so I can tend his wound. He'll never wake up if he doesn't get some care."

"You'll run away."

"I won't leave my brother."

"I don't trust you, but I will loosen the rope on your hands."

"Untie Diego. He needs rest. He can't relax, tied the way he is."

"He should be rested. He's been asleep long enough."

"And he needs food. Without food he'll be weak. Do you want it said you starve your enemies so they have no strength to fight you?"

Black Bear gave a muffled growl. "You talk too much, Estrella."

Through half-lidded eyes I watched him rearrange her bindings. He said, "I'll send food and water, but he will remain tied." Then he left the wickiup.

Estrella sighed. "He's gone."

I opened my eyes and looked around the hut. The only opening was the door. "Do they ever let you outside?"

"Once in the morning and once in the evening, but there is always someone with me."

"What direction does the wickiup face?"

"The center. The huts are built in a circle."

"Have you seen my horse?"

"No, but I've seen Bonita. What are you thinking?"

"We have to escape, Estrella. But we need El Cid and my weapons."

I heard footsteps. "Someone's coming." I closed my eyes.

"Hello, Spotted Fawn," said Estrella. "Is it time for my walk already?"

"If you like. Black Bear sent this."

Through my eyelashes I saw the Indian girl set down two baskets. Then she spoke again. "Does Black Bear want you for his wife?"

"No, Spotted Fawn, he does not. He says I talk too much."

"But he likes to look at you. He comes here all the time."

"It's not me," Estrella said. "He's waiting for my brother to wake up. Then I don't know what he has in mind. I think he'll send me home."

"This man who wears a snake hat is your brother?"

"Yes."

"When your brother's wound is healed Black Bear will send you away?"

"Yes, I'm sure of it."

Spotted Fawn shuffled her feet as though undecided

about something. The fine dust she stirred tickled my nose, and I pressed my face into the sheepskin to keep from sneezing. "Then I'll help you," she said. "I brought some tule, sprinkle it on his wound."

I knew that the Apache used pollen of the cattail plant, or tule, to heal wounds and thanked the saints that Spotted Fawn was jealous of Estrella. With medicine, my head would heal faster.

"Thank you, Spotted Fawn," Estrella said. "After I tend to my brother, could we go for our walk?"

"If you like." Spotted Fawn sat on the ground and cut Estrella's bonds with a knife.

"Will you loosen my brother too?"

"No." Spotted Fawn settled herself to wait. "Hurry," she said.

Estrella tore a piece from her petticoat and washed the blood from my head. She sprinkled the yellow pollen on the wound and wrapped my head with another scrap of her underskirt.

"Come," Spotted Fawn said, "Now I will take you on your walk."

When the girls were away from the wickiup, I tried to sit up. My hands were tied behind my back and my feet tied at the ankles. I pushed against the dirt floor with my hands and pulled myself to a sitting position. I looked around the bare hut and decided I could kick through the flimsy walls made of dried twigs and sticks.

My mind filled with thoughts of escape, I glanced around the wickiup. One of the baskets held dried meat, the other water. My large knife was gone. I prayed Black Bear had not found my boot knife.

The Cucuri had told me about the courage and cunning

of the Apache when trailing an enemy. Stripped to a loincloth and knee-high moccasins, their only weapons a bow, a quiver of arrows, and a knife, the Apache warrior would ride his horse to exhaustion. Then he'd butcher it, attach strips of its meat to a long stick to dry in the sun, cut a length of the intestine, fill it with water, drape it around his neck, and carrying the drying meat, continue on the trail on foot, not stopping for rest.

To escape Black Bear and his tribe, I would need the skill and bravery of my enemy.

At the sound of Estrella's voice, I flopped down on the sheepskin. She talked without pause as the girls entered the wickiup. "Black Bear is right," Spotted Fawn said. "You talk so much my brain is addled. Sit down so I can tie you up."

"Don't forget to keep the binds loose so I can tend my brother's wound."

"I can't listen to you anymore. I go now and won't be back until morning," Spotted Fawn said and left the wickiup.

Estrella sighed and whispered, "How are you, Diego?"

"A lot better," I said and sat up. "Did you see El Cid?"

"Yes. He is tied to a tree on the other side of the village. Spotted Fawn told me that all the warriors want him, and Black Bear is going to sell him to the highest bidder. The warriors are gathering their belongings for the trade that is to take place tonight."

"All right. We have to escape tonight then." I stretched my legs as far as I could. "Can you reach into my right boot? Yes, there. Is my knife still there?"

"Yes!" Estrella pulled out the knife.

I turned my back. "Now cut my wrists loose. Wait. I

hear someone coming." I fell back onto the sheepskin.

Black Bear strode into the wickiup. He glared down at me. "I see you're finally awake."

CHAPTER 13

FROM THE CORNER of my eye, I saw Estrella slip the knife into her skirt pocket.

With the tip of his knife, Black Bear tore my shirt open. "This is just a sample of the evening's entertainment."

Estrella struggled to stand. "What are you doing, Black Bear? Diego is helpless. Turn him loose so he can fight you."

I caught her eye and shook my head. She settled back, head on her knees. Black Bear sneered. "Ever the loving sister, I see."

He frowned at me; his black eyes burned with hate. "You always wanted to be Storm Cloud." He hefted his knife, and then in a sudden movement he traced a jagged line across my chest. His glittering eyes never left mine. I clenched my teeth and stared back without blinking. Drops of blood made a zigzag pattern on my breast.

"He's bleeding," Estrella cried. "Cut me loose so I can tend his wound."

Black Bear snickered. "There's not so much blood.

He'll bleed much more later; I can promise you that." He strode out without looking back, and we were alone again.

"Quick, Estrella, get the knife. We have to get out of here right now."

"You're bleeding. I'll have to put some medicine on it."

"Never mind that now. We don't have much time. Cut the bindings."

She sawed on the rawhide until the bindings loosened. I stretched my hands apart and the ties separated. "Good." I rubbed circulation into my wrists and hands.

My fingers fumbled as I untied Estrella's bonds. "I'm being careful because we're going to need these straps." I loosened our ankles and stepped out of my leather chaps. "Put these on."

She struggled into the chaps and her dress bunched up around her waist. "My skirt is in the way. Why do I need these chaps?"

"We're going into rough country. The mesquite thorns prick and can cause poison." I thought for a minute and remembered Father talking about a divided skirt for Estrella. "Take off your petticoat and slit your skirt up the middle, back and front."

When she'd done that, we wrapped the ends of her skirt around her legs. The chaps covered her to the ankles. She wore sturdy shoes, so I could only hope for the best.

Her pockets were two cotton squares tied around her waist under her skirt, I filled both with dried meat. With the strings, I tied one bundle around Estrella's waist and one around mine. "Drink as much water as you can," I said. "There is nothing here to carry water in." I stuffed the packet of tule in my pocket with the remains of the cotton petticoat and looked around for any other useful article. There was nothing. I tucked my knife in its boot sheath and tied the hat strings under my chin.

I peeked out the door. The sun had set and painted the blue sky with pink and coral and purple. We needed to leave soon, before they started the bidding for El Cid.

"You'll have to show me where they have the horses," I said. "Do you know where Bonita is?" She nodded. I doubted the little mare could keep the pace of my strong and tireless horse, but a double burden would slow down El Cid, and Bonita was swift. We might find a hiding place before she tired.

"You may have to ride bareback," I told Estrella.

"That's all right. Don't worry about me. I'll hang on, no matter what."

We had to leave before dusk turned into night. I kicked a hole into the brush wall in the back of the wickiup. With my hand I enlarged it. "Can you get out?"

She slipped out with no difficulty. I wriggled my shoulders through and pulled myself out. I looked up at the heavens to get my bearings. The stars were not yet out. In the east, a pale, silver moon floated in the lavender sky. Estrella took my hand and led me to the horses.

CHAPTER 14
Escape

THROUGH MESQUITE AND sagebrush, we skirted the village to where Bonita and El Cid were tied in a line with the Apache horses. Their braided buffalo hair halters were fastened to a rawhide rope stretched between two juniper trees.

I pressed my hand over El Cid's nose to prevent his welcoming nicker and stroked his face. I helped Estrella mount Bonita, then slashed one end of the rawhide line and cut our horses loose. "Lay flat against Bonita's neck," I whispered, "and hang on to her mane. We'll be moving very fast."

I cut the other end of the tether line and holding it and Bonita's lead in one hand, bounded onto El Cid's back. I leaned forward and whispered in his ear, "Go, boy, now!" and touched his flanks with my heels.

My gallant steed hurtled down the rocky hillside with the other horses running behind him. Over the thudding hooves I heard shouting but didn't turn to look. I prayed the Apache would think that the horses had broken loose.

I glanced at my sister. Her face set in grim determination, she clung to Bonita's back. The little mare galloped gamely beside El Cid. The shouting faded in the distance.

To my right I heard an outcry. This time I turned my head. A lone warrior stood on a high rock gesturing with his lance, his horse beside him—the lookout. I'd forgotten about the scout. Arrows hummed over our heads. "Stay down," I shouted, and nudged El Cid to run faster.

We galloped for another two leagues, and I sensed that Bonita was faltering. Her hide was flecked with foam. I slowed the pace gradually to a lope and then to a canter. I looked the Apache ponies over and spotted a large black stallion with white socks on his hind legs. I brought the string of horses to a walk and led them into a stand of trees. I dismounted and helped Estrella down. The horses shook their heads, snorted, and blew air. They smelled of heat and sweat.

"We have to leave Bonita," I said. "She can't run anymore, but she is so brave she'll die trying."

"What will happen to her if we leave her?"

"When she is rested, she'll find her way home. She'll probably follow us for a while, but she's too tired to go far."

"I don't want anything bad to happen to her." Estrella picked up a handful of grass and wiped the lather from the heaving sides of her horse.

"We'll leave her here with the other horses." I removed the halters from all but the black horse. Neither he nor El Cid had broken into a sweat from the long hard run. The thought crossed my mind that this might be one of

Father's experimental horses. If so, he could keep pace with El Cid and we'd be home by this time tomorrow.

"We have to hurry," I said. "That Apache scout may be right behind us." I helped Estrella onto the black, coiled the rawhide tether-line around my shoulders and vaulted onto El Cid.

The blue-black sky held few stars and the half-moon glowed with a dim light. I started the horses at a lope. They appeared fresh from the short rest, and I set them to a gallop. I knew Estrella was tired, but she didn't complain, and we had to get as far from Apache territory as we could.

The rocks loomed large and cast grotesque shadows in the dark. Clumps of deformed shrubs and bushes huddled in the night, but the horses dodged the greasewood and saltbush and ran with a steady, pounding gait.

A black, wavering line of an arroyo suddenly appeared in our path. I hadn't time to slow the horses, so nudged El Cid and with the rawhide rope, slapped the black on his rump. El Cid bunched his muscles and jumped over the arroyo. The black never broke stride and landed on the other side of the ditch beside him. I laughed at the thrill and turned to Estrella. She wasn't on the horse. I wheeled our mounts and went back to the arroyo. I didn't see her.

"Estrella, where are you?"

"Here, I'm down here." Her voice sounded faint and distant.

I slid from my horse, skidded down the steep sides of the arroyo, and created a small landslide with the dislodged rocks and clumps of dirt. Estrella sat in a crumpled heap on the floor of the arroyo.

"Are you hurt?" I helped her stand.

"My right leg. It hurts to put my foot down."

"We have to get out of here. Lean on me." I put my arm around her waist and half carried and half dragged her up the slope made by the landslide. "You have to try and ride." I set her on the black horse. She slumped over and swayed. I feared that she would fall so I held on to El Cid's reins and hopped up behind her. "Hold onto the mane. I'll find a place for us to rest." She shivered as though cold, and I removed my jacket and helped her into it.

The forbidding landscape offered little in the way of shelter or protection. To the west, a mesa towered over the others. The blue mesa I'd seen every day of my life loomed black in the fading moonlight. I turned the horses and we plodded toward the mountain with the strange rock formation. There we could hide behind rocks. Maybe there would be a cave and, hopefully, water.

CHAPTER 15
The Blue Mesa

NIGHT HAD PALED into daylight by the time we reached the foothill. I slipped off the horse and, holding Estrella upright, led the horses up the rocky slope. We skirted boulders and stunted pines, and as the sun topped the horizon, I found an alcove formed by large rocks.

I helped Estrella from the horse, and she sat on a rock with her head in her hands. I checked her leg. Her ankle was swollen with purple and blue bruises. "It might be broken, Estrella. I'll do what I can and we'll rest the day here, but we must get back to the ranch soon. I'm worried the Indians will attack and Father will need my help."

"I'll be ready to ride in a bit, Diego. Just let me rest for a while." She sank to the ground and lay curled against the rock.

I found a patch of grass and let the horses graze. Then I scouted the area for better shelter. Higher up the mesa I saw an opening in the rock. I crawled through and found myself in a large cave. Several rooms branched off from the main cavern. The rock floor was clean, as though recently swept. There were no cobwebs or bat droppings and no sign of habitation, either human or animal.

I turned to the sound of water. In a corner of the cave, a thin stream dripped into a small pond. Sunbeams reflected off the water from a hole in the roof. I dipped my hand in the pool. The water tasted cool and sweet.

From my pocket I took a scrap of Estrella's petticoat and moistened it. I crawled through the tunnel and pressed the wet rag against her lips. She sucked on the cloth and opened her pain-filled eyes. "Thanks, Diego, that helps a lot."

"I found a cave with water in it, but I don't know if you can crawl through the opening. Let me fix a brace for your leg and then we'll try it." I broke off two branches from a pine and peeled bark from the sides with my boot knife until the limb was slick and smooth. I helped Estrella step out of my chaps, placed a branch on each side of her ankle and tied it to her leg with strips from her underskirt.

With my small knife I chopped boughs from the pines and dragged them into the cave. Then I spread my leather chaps over the limbs. The fragrance of pine filled the cavern. "All right," I said, "I made you a bed in the cave, I'll help you through."

When we were inside the cave, Estrella looked around. "This is very nice. I think I'll have some more water." She crawled to the pool and drank, then sank onto her pine bough bed. "And now, I'm going to rest."

"Why don't you have some jerky? We haven't eaten since yesterday, and you need your strength." My own stomach growled from hunger.

We each took a piece of meat, and as I chewed, I worked out how I'd get water to the horses. After Estrella closed her eyes in fatigue and I covered her with my leather jacket, I filled my hat with the precious fluid. Both horses grazed in contentment but looked gaunt from lack of water. I offered my hat to El Cid and he plunged his nose in but before he drank it all, I gave the remainder to the black. "You need a name," I told him. "Because you are a brave and handsome horse, I think I'll call you *Guapo*." I scratched the white star on his forehead and he butted me in the chest.

Four times I filled my hat before I satisfied the horses' thirst. I climbed to a high rock and surveyed the plains below. I picked up a piece of sandstone and sharpened my little knife. I pulled my sombrero low on my face, leaned back against a boulder and chewed on another piece of jerky.

CHAPTER 16

I HAD NO weapons, only my boot-knife. If the Apache attacked us, they would come armed with lances and the bows and arrows they'd made. I, too, could make a bow.

I broke off a straight limb from a pine tree and with my knife I smoothed and whittled it into the shape of a bow. I notched each end, and for a bowstring fitted it with a length of our rawhide bindings. I tested the pull and decided the bow might work, although the string was thick. The Indians used sinew for bowstrings, but I had only dry rawhide. Making an arrow proved more difficult.

I peeled straight sticks with my knife and notched one end to fit the bowstring. I searched for feathers but found none and for the first time realized that I heard no birds twittering in the trees, no crows cawing in defiance, and no insects buzzing. There were no tracks or sign of bird or animal of any kind except for that of our horses. And there was no breeze. I thought this a strange circumstance but pushed it from my mind as I searched for flint to knap into an arrowhead. I found nothing but granite and sandstone so in the end shaped two sticks into sharp points and then took up my post on the lookout rock.

While I mused on the absence of animals, a swirl of sand on the plain caught my eye and a band of Indians emerged from the dust cloud. I flattened myself on the rock and heaved a sigh of relief when the Indians proved to be a group of Tewa. They were not trailing us and their ponies would erase our horses' tracks. But then my mind twisted with worry when I saw that they headed south—toward my father's ranch, and I could do nothing to help defend our hacienda.

I crawled into the cave where Estrella slept curled on her side. Color had returned to her face and the pain lines erased from her brow.

Behind the waterfall, sunbeams dappled the rock wall with glistening streaks. I ran my hand over the uneven face of the rock and with my knife dug a fist-sized lump of the glossy substance from the stone. It had a silvery sheen and was softer than the rock. The tip of my knife broke off, but I dug out three almost identical smaller pieces and shoved them in my pocket.

I stepped out into the sunshine and sat on my lookout rock, the silence so thick and heavy it weighed on me like a buffalo robe. I examined my shiny stone. It had a rough texture and mixed with the shiny chunks were bits of black. I rubbed the stone on my woolen trousers. It glittered in the sunlight and I knew I'd found an abundant source of silver ore. I examined my broken knife with sadness. It had served me well. I determined to hone and sharpen the blade until the tip was again pointed and slipped it into my boot.

I turned my attention to the plains below and spotted another group of Indians. From their dress and manner of riding I knew these were Apache. Flat on my stomach, I held my breath and reached for my bow and arrows, but the Indians didn't appear aware of my presence, but I watched until they disappeared from view before I breathed easy again.

A pebble bounced down the hillside sounding loud in the stillness. I turned my head and saw a shadow. I rolled onto my back. Black Bear stood over me, crouched, knife held high, ready to pounce.

He bared his teeth and lunged. "You can't escape me now, Spanish dog."

I rolled to the side, grabbed his upraised arm with my left hand and jabbed him in the chest with my pointed stick. His knife pierced my left arm near the shoulder, but I scarcely felt the pain or the warm wetness that soaked my shirt. I bounded to my feet and longed for my sword. He rushed at me again. I stepped aside, made a futile stab with my stick and he laughed.

Black Bear was taller and heavier than I, but I was quicker. I maneuvered myself until I stood with my back against a large rock. When he charged, I braced myself against the rock and kicked him, high and hard. I aimed for the groin, but my foot landed in his stomach. He grunted and dropped the knife. He grabbed me around the shoulders and wrestled me to the ground. I drew my knees to my chest and pushed him off. I bounced to my feet. Swift as a lizard he came at me, his face twisted with rage and hate. We grappled among the rocks until, together, we fell to the dirt. We rolled closer and closer to the edge of the mesa as we scuffled. I wriggled and squirmed, but his fury gave him strength and he held me in a vise-like grip around the rib cage. I couldn't get away. I reached out on the ground and my right hand found a rock. It was the silver ore. I smashed it against his head. It shattered into pieces. Bits of silver glittered in the sun.

The blow dazed Black Bear for a moment but it didn't stop him. He rushed at me in a wild rage and clutched me around the throat. Blood from his wound dripped onto my face. His thumbs pressed into my windpipe. "At last I will have avenged my father," he said through clenched teeth. I struggled and gasped for breath.

Through a red mist I saw Estrella. With both hands she held a dried tree limb over her head. She didn't hesitate. She struck Black Bear across his shoulders. It must have knocked the wind out of him because he staggered to his feet, looked around with wild eyes, and muttered something in a language I didn't understand.

I stood, stroked my neck, breathed deep, and filled my lungs with the good air. With outstretched arms, Black Bear took one menacing step toward Estrella. I moved in front of her and lifted a hand. "No! Black Bear, no! We are not the ones responsible for your parents' death."

"All you Spanish dogs are responsible," he roared and rushed at us. In his blind rage, he didn't see the shriveled root of a dead tree. The root caught his foot and he tottered on the edge of the mesa. Instinctively I reached out to stop his fall.

He jerked away from me and toppled backward. His scream ripped the still air. Neither Estrella nor I said a word as in horror we watched his body bounce down the hillside. It hit boulders with mushy thuds and broke tree limbs with resounding crashes. As one, we turned and walked to the rock alcove.

"I should climb down and see how badly he's hurt," I said. But in my heart, I knew there was nothing I could do for him; it was a long way to the bottom of the mesa.

"You're hurt, Diego. I'll make a bandage for you first, and then I'll ride down with you." She shook her head and clicked her tongue. "If we keep getting wounded like this, we're going to use up my entire petticoat."

I pulled out the cotton scraps and the packet of cattail pollen. "Put the tule on the cut, it healed my head." With the broken blade of my knife, I tore off the blood-soaked sleeve of my shirt. Then I cut off the other sleeve. "We can use this to wash the blood off." I examined the slash. "But I don't think the cut is too deep." The blood from the mark on my chest had dried into a thin jagged line.

Estrella limped up the path to the cave and I could see that every step caused her pain. She needed more rest. I climbed the rocky trail and sat by the entrance. "I don't think there is much we can do for Black Bear, we might as well stay here," I said.

"I know," she answered, "but we have to at least try."

Estrella tended my wound. "I'm ready to ride now, if you like," she said.

With my dampened shirt sleeve, I cleaned the blood off my face. "There's no hurry. Indians are riding back and forth down there and some of them are Apache. It would be better if we stay here the rest of the day. I'll water the horses and then after the sun sets, we'll ride down the mesa. After we do what we can for Black Bear we'll travel all night. With luck we'll be home by morning."

CHAPTER 17

ESTRELLA SAT WITH me on the lookout rock. We chewed on some jerky and talked about Black Bear. We both knew there was nothing we could do for him, but my blood boiled when she told me how he had kidnapped her.

"Listen," she said.

"I know," I said. "The silence. It's eerie, in a pleasant kind of way. It's strange there is no wind and no birds or insects up here."

"There are some birds." She pointed to the sky where turkey buzzards had begun to gather. They had spotted Black Bear's body. The voiceless black birds circled lower and lower until they flew so close, we could see their red heads and curved yellow beaks.

A bay horse rounded a large boulder at the foot of the mesa. "It's Bonita," Estrella said. We lost sight of the horse as it turned up the mesa trail. A man on horseback followed the mare. "And White Wolf." Estrella's eyes sparkled with happiness. I, too, was glad to see White Wolf.

The two horses trudged up the mesa. Their hooves rang loud in the stillness. The path was steep and rocky, so I knew White Wolf would dismount before he rounded the bend. Bonita came in sight first, then White Wolf leading his horse and a brown and white spotted pony saddled with my gear.

A look of relief flooded his face when White Wolf caught sight of us. "This is Black Bear's horse, and I feared the worst when I saw the vultures," he said.

"How did you find us?" asked Estrella.

"I followed Bonita. At first, I thought she was headed home, but when she turned west, I hoped she was trailing you."

Estrella took White Wolf by the hand. "Diego said she'd follow us after she rested. Come, sit down. Tell us where you've been."

He shook his head and smiled. "You first."

She laid her head on his shoulder and told him of our escape from the Apache camp. His arm stole around her waist, and I was happy for my sister and for White Wolf.

When Estrella came to the part about our fight with Black Bear, White Wolf tightened his arm around her and turned to me. "Then Black Bear no longer lives?"

"No, I don't think so." I pointed to the vultures. "But I must climb down and do what I can for him."

White Wolf shook his head. "Black Bear is beyond any help, but you are still in serious danger."

"Yes, as are our parents. We plan on leaving here after dark. Can you tell me where the Apache are camped? I have no doubt I can defeat them."

White Wolf raised his eyebrows in question, so I told him of my vision.

"The Pueblos have started a full-scale war and no Spaniard is safe. I stopped at my village and our medicine man, Owl Feather, made medicine over this as a charm to protect you." White Wolf took out Estrella's sapphire pendant and clasped it around her neck. "I will travel with you and you should be safe from the Indians. But it is not my people that I am concerned about, Diego. Do you not know where you are?"

"I don't know the name, but it's the blue mesa we can see from your pueblo and from our hacienda."

"This is one of the sacred mountains of the Tewa. No one ever comes here; it is dangerous."

Estrella looked around in admiration. "So, this is the mysterious blue mesa. I've always wanted to come here. It's not dangerous. I slept in the cave up there all morning and no harm came to me." She pointed to the cave entrance. "And the water in the lake is cool and sweet." White Wolf paled. "You must never go in there again. Women especially are not allowed in the labyrinths of a sacred mesa."

"Why?" I asked. "Why is it dangerous to enter the cave?"

"There is a strong wind that whistles through the tunnels and caves. The elders tell of people who have been swept away by the wind and are never seen again. Lame Deer came here two moons ago. He has not returned to the pueblo."

"There is no wind in the cavern. Listen." I held up my hand. "Hear that? There is nothing, no wind, not even a bird chirping."

"That's because they've all been carried away by the wind."

I remembered Chief Leaping Antelope talking to Father about Lame Deer and began to feel uneasy. It was not natural that there were no animals on the mesa, not even a lizard or a spider, so there might be some truth to the legend. "All right, White Wolf," I said, "we'll not go in the cave again, only for water."

"What happens to the people who get caught in the wind?" asked Estrella.

"No one knows. They may be sucked down into the bowels of the earth, down to the beginning of time, where the ancestors of our people once lived. Or maybe they go where the winds live, into the four corners of the earth."

"Do you know of a water hole between here and the ranch?" I did not want to go back into the cave.

"No," White Wolf said. "There is no water within a day's ride."

I took a deep breath. "Then I'll have to use the water from the cave for the horses."

"If the wind blows," he said, "don't go near the entrance."

"I'll be careful, White Wolf, but the horses need water." I went to Black Bear's horse and took the water bag from my saddle. I thanked the saints my sword was in its sheath and my blanket tied behind the cantle, but Gaspar's musket was missing.

CHAPTER 18
The Whirlwind

WE HAD FIVE horses to water, so I needed a better bowl than my hat. I scouted around until I found a large sandstone with a natural depression. It probably held water during the rainy season, but it would take many trips with the water flask to fill the basin with enough water for the horses.

White Wolf brought his water bag. "I'll help. We don't need all the horses. We'll water only the two we are going to use."

"Three," I said.

"No, Rainbow will ride with me."

"Then we'll take the two best horses, El Cid and Guapo." I pointed to the black. The other horses would have to fend for themselves.

White Wolf nodded and put his saddle on Guapo and mine on El Cid. "Promise me this, Diego, no matter what happens, you will go on to the ranch and help your family.

I will care for Estrella, and she wears the charm, so she is safe."

"No, White Wolf, it's safer for us to ride together. Besides what could happen?"

He glanced toward the cave entrance with a worried look. "We might get separated."

"Guapo is a strong horse. He can keep pace with El Cid. We won't get separated."

"Even so, promise me. And I make this vow to you: I will stay by Estrella's side always. I will never leave her and will protect her with my life."

"Is this what you want, Estrella?" I asked. "Do you want to ride with White Wolf?"

"Yes," she said, and the tender look that passed between them made me avert my eyes. I felt I was seeing something sacred and private.

"Very well then, White Wolf, I give you my sister." I placed her hand in his. "And if something happens so that I cannot continue, you must promise to leave me and deliver Estrella safely to the ranch."

White Wolf agreed and we clasped wrists. I took the water bags and squirmed into the tunnel. Estrella crawled in behind me. "I want to help," she said. "I'll stay in here and fill the flasks. You carry them to the horses. It will save time. Your shoulders are so broad it takes you forever to wiggle through that small opening."

"All right." I took the filled bags and turned to go out the cave. White Wolf blocked my exit.

"You should not be in here, Estrella," he said. "You know how dangerous it is."

"Not for me," she said. "I've been in here all morning, and besides I want to help."

White Wolf caught my eye. I shrugged. "You know how stubborn she is."

"I'll stay in here with her, then. But hurry." He moved from the opening.

I took the filled bags and poured the water into the sandstone basin. I hurried back to the cave. White Wolf took them from me and returned with the full bags. Twice more we relayed the water flasks. I returned the third time and said, "Fill these for our use and come on out of the cave. I'll water the horses and we can leave the mesa."

I led El Cid and Guapo to the water and went back to the cave. I stuck my head in the opening and said, "Put my chaps on, Estrella, and wear my jacket. If an Indian gets sight of you, maybe he'll think you're a man."

"That's a good idea." White Wolf helped Estrella with the chaps. She shoved her arms into the jacket sleeves just as a long wailing cry echoed through the cavern. "Go, Diego, hurry." White Wolf picked up Estrella and carried her to the opening.

I crawled from the tunnel, grasped Estrella by the wrists and pulled her out. White Wolf was right behind her. A strong wind shrieked through the mouth of the tunnel and knocked us to the ground. I scrambled to my feet. White Wolf carried Estrella in his arms. We ran to the horses and I grabbed the reins. With a loud crash, the pine bough bed tumbled out of the cave and the wind blew the branches over the edge of the mesa. The gale turned into a whirlwind. With a loud howl it gyrated toward us. The horses neighed and reared. I held the reins tight to their muzzles and tried to calm them. They shook their heads, snorted and rolled their eyes until they showed white. Braying and kicking, the horses backed away and pulled me with them.

White Wolf shouted, "I have Guapo, go, Diego, go."

I vaulted into the saddle and El Cid sprang into a gallop. The other three horses ran headlong down the mountainside, their manes and tails streamed behind like banners. Trees bent to the ground from the force of the gale. The wind screeched and tore at my shirt. My hat blew off and somersaulted off rocks and over trees. I slowed El Cid and turned in the saddle.

White Wolf and my sister sat on Guapo. The wind-storm coiled around them and spiraled upward until it formed a funnel. In the center of the whirlwind the horse bucked and pitched. White Wolf bent over Estrella, protecting her with his body while he tried to control the frightened horse. I raced back and reached out to help, but the heavy wind pushed against me and I couldn't penetrate the invisible shield. Guapo reared and pawed at the cocoon of air. He stretched his neck toward me, I grasped his bridle and together El Cid and I pulled. I yanked and tugged until the terrified horses broke free of the whirlwind.

Guapo galloped down the hill with White Wolf and Estrella clinging to his back. The wind whirled around me and off the mesa sweeping away rocks and loose limbs. I urged El Cid to a gallop, but the wind buffeted us so strongly he could not move forward. My brave horse tossed his head and snorted. His body quivered and I could smell his fear. I thought to dismount and help pull him through the storm, but in horror saw that we floated ten feet off the ground.

Suddenly, with a deafening roar we were twisting and spinning through the air. I could see nothing but swirls of gray against the blue sky. Dirt filled my nostrils and sand gritted against my teeth. I looked down. The blue mesa was nothing but a speck of red rock amid clouds of dust.

It shames me to admit that the wind swept away my courage and I had no thought for Estrella or White Wolf and if they had escaped the whirlwind. I thought only of my own safety and had no words of comfort for El Cid. I clung tightly to the saddle, shut my eyes against the stinging wind, and wondered where the storm was taking me.

CHAPTER 19
2021 – The Future

SOMETHING TOUCHED MY shoulder, and I realized that I was no longer spinning in the air but lying in cool grass, my hand gripping the bridle reins and El Cid nosing my body. I opened my eyes to see unfamiliar faces peering at me. I leaped onto El Cid and drew my sword.

A man, I took for the leader, spoke in a harsh voice and gestured with authority. The people stepped back, but there were too many to fight so I sheathed my sword and nudged El Cid. The people surrounded us. We could find no opening to flee.

I glanced at each member in the group. They numbered twenty-five, male and female, all about my age, and carried no weapons that I could see. They did not look dangerous but wore odd looking clothes and didn't belong to any tribe with which I was familiar. I would take no chances.

The sun reflected off the leader's round, dark eyes. No

whites showed, and I could not read the expression in his eyes. About my father's age, he had no beard, only a mustache and short black hair. Two women stood to the side with the same kind of eyes as the leader.

One woman reached up, removed her eyes, held them in her hand, and rubbed them with a small white cloth. Underneath those dark disks, her eyes appeared normal and it occurred to me that perhaps those dark circles were a mark that only their chiefs wore.

These people all stared at me with shock written on their faces, and I knew I was as much a surprise to them as they were to me. They talked among themselves in a language I had never heard. I understood Latin and knew many words in several of the Indian dialects. Perhaps they spoke in the Greek that Father Marcos planned to teach me.

Many thoughts whirled in my head, but the only thing clear was that the wind brought me here. Where I was, I could not say. Nothing looked familiar. We stood in a meadow beside a small stream lined with cottonwoods. A wooden building with a large wheel spanned the creek. An irrigation ditch led from the waterway to the fields below.

I scanned the horizon and with a thrill recognized the blue mesa. The sight calmed me and I glanced at the sky. The sun was at the mid-day mark. With luck I could reach the blue mesa before nightfall. I nudged El Cid to a slow walk to pass through the press of people.

The leader said something, reached out and grabbed El Cid's bridle. My horse snorted, shook his head, and reared. He slashed out with his forefeet and the leader jumped back.

Although I did not think he could understand me, I

said, "Do not touch my horse again, Señor. He is a trained warhorse and trusts no one. Allow us to pass, please."

"I'm sorry," he said, "but you look as though you've either been hurt in a fight or you are an expert makeup artist. Tell us about your role here at the museum."

The accent on his Spanish words was different from mine, but I had no difficulty understanding him. "I know nothing of a museum."

"Aren't you a part of this living museum? Your costume is the most authentic I've seen."

"I do not comprehend what you say, Señor. I have to go now, please allow me to pass."

"Where do you come from? I've heard that up to about one hundred years ago, people in the more isolated areas spoke in the Spanish you use."

For some reason, his words bothered me. My stomach clenched and jumbled thoughts filled my brain so that I could not think. A girl came and stood beside the leader. "No one will harm you. Please let us help." She spoke in a gentle voice that somehow sounded familiar. Her long blonde hair and serene blue eyes reminded me of someone I trusted. "What is your name?" she asked.

I had to remain calm and get my thoughts in order so I could escape. Before answering, I glanced at the curious faces that surrounded me, and once again noticed that these people carried no visible weapons, but most had saddlebags on their backs. "My name is Diego Francisco Montez y Montera."

"My name is Hector Alvarado," the leader said. "I am a history teacher and this is my class. We are here at this living museum to learn how the Spanish settlers of the eighteenth and nineteenth centuries lived. Are you sure you're not a part of this museum?"

I shook my head.

"Most of my class is also studying the Spanish language," the teacher said. "So even if you cannot speak English, we can still communicate."

Every word he spoke confused me, but I was becoming accustomed to hearing strange words and had questions of my own. "How many leagues to the blue mesa?"

It was the teacher's turn to look confused. "I do not know the blue mesa." I pointed northeast. "That mesa... over there."

"Oh, that one. About thirty miles. We are about fifty miles southwest of Santa Fe."

"My home is fifteen leagues south of Santa Fe."

"One league is equal to almost three miles, so you're in the vicinity of your home. Why don't you get off that horse and have some lunch with us?"

I glanced down at the smiling and friendly faces. "Come on, Diego," one of the boys said. "My name is Jared and I have more than enough for the both of us." He spoke slowly and hesitated before each word.

I appreciated their hospitality and since I'd had nothing to eat but a piece of jerky since morning, I dismounted and tied El Cid to a cottonwood branch. I brushed my hand across my leg and a dust cloud rose in the air.

"Whoa, man, where you been?" my new friend asked.

Suddenly, I became aware of my tattered shirt, my dusty and bloodstained clothes. "I got caught in a windstorm."

Another boy strode toward me, hand outstretched. "Hi, I'm Jason."

"Hello." I clasped his wrist.

"Cool," Jason said. His clear gray eyes twinkled.

"And I'm Zach," another boy said. "Would you like a banana?"

I stared at the yellow and brown object he offered. It resembled a gourd but smelled and looked like nothing I'd ever seen, and I shook my head.

"We'll just spread our combined lunches out and you can pick whatever you'd like," Jared said.

I stared at the food they placed on the grass. There was an orange ball, bread in clear containers, and the thing Zach called a banana. Then I saw the only thing I recognized—an apple. I reached for it and noticed my dirt covered hand. I went to the creek and washed, cupped my hand to drink some water.

"I wouldn't drink from that river," Zach said. "It's the Rio Grande."

I looked at the shallow, slow moving stream. "It can't be. The Rio Grande runs wide and deep. This is little more than a creek."

"It's the Rio Grande. Try this." He offered me a metal container. "It's a coke."

I examined the object. It had no opening, only a ring on one end.

"This is how you open it." Zach inserted a finger in the ring and pulled.

I did the same and carefully watched my new friends drink from their containers. I lifted the cup and sipped. The liquid tickled my tongue, but it tasted cool and sweet. I wanted to see this strange drink and poured some on the grass. The brown liquid foamed—much like the froth on a frog pond. How could something that looked like scum taste so pleasant?

I glanced at my three new friends, their faces so friendly and open that I wanted to trust them. Maybe they could answer some questions. "Can you tell me anything about the Pueblo Rebellion?"

"We studied the one that happened back in 1680 during the seventeenth century," Jared said. "What do you want to know?"

"Isn't that the one that Mr. Alvarado said was the only war that the Indians ever won?" Jason asked.

"Yes," Zach said. "They chased every Spaniard out of New Mexico. For twelve years, not one white man was left in the territory."

Even my lips felt numb. "What happened to the Spaniards?" My voice sounded faint.

"Those that weren't killed were allowed to go south to Mexico."

They talked of the rebellion as though it happened many years ago. "What year is this?"

They glanced at one another, questions in their eyes. "You don't know the year? Where you been man?"

"Please. I must know. At least tell me the century."

"We're into the twenty-first century. Why? What's going on with you?"

Every Spaniard banished or killed. My shoulders sagged, my stomach churned, my limbs went weak as a newborn lamb. "I have to get to the blue mesa right away so I can go home."

"Where's home?"

"The seventeenth century," I whispered. "1680." From the look on their faces, I could tell they didn't believe me. In truth, I hardly believed it myself. They chattered together in their own language while my brain whirled with questions. I worried about my sister. Had she escaped the whirlwind? I worried about my family. Were they safe from the Indians?

I hadn't noticed that the blonde girl had joined us until she spoke. "Tell us what happened, Diego."

"This is my sister, Kylie," Jason said. "Yes, tell us what happened, we want to help you."

I told them about the whirlwind and that to my mind the only way for me to return home was to let the wind take me. "I think your teacher suspects something and wants to detain me. Can you distract him until I can ride away?"

"You can't ride horseback to the blue mesa from here," Zach said. "There are too many obstacles."

"I can find my way. I've ridden farther than that many times."

Jared shook his head. "You don't understand, Diego. There are towns filled with people, freeways crowded with cars and trucks. We'll take you there in a horse trailer."

I must have looked confused because he smiled. "Don't worry about anything. We'll find someplace to hide you and your horse and come back for you tonight."

"We can't leave Diego here," Kylie said. "He's been hurt. We'll have to take him to our home and care for his wounds. He probably should see a doctor."

"No," I said. "My wounds are nothing. I cannot take the time for a doctor. My family is in danger and I must get home quickly."

Jason nodded. "Okay. No doctor, but you can go with us to our house. Our mother is one of the chaperones and has her own car. She drives a van so there's enough room for all of us, but we will have to leave the horse. I'll go talk to her, the rest of you find a place for the horse." And he ran to where his mother sat with the other woman and the teacher.

"I will not leave El Cid."

But the others explained that my horse would be safer here until we could return for him. The time, they said, would be short because a car could run faster than any horse. This idea intrigued me, and, in the end, they convinced me. I led El Cid deeper into the cottonwoods and unsaddled him. My friends assured me he would be safe here as the museum was about to close for the day and the visitors would all have to leave.

Still, I worried, and when my horse nickered and followed me out of the trees, I realized that the strange happenings made him nervous too. "I will stay here with my horse and when it is dark, we will go to the blue mesa."

Nothing they said could sway me in my decision, and finally Jared said, "Then I'll wait with you. It will take two or three hours for them to get back and the time will pass more quickly if there are two of us."

He spoke in his own language to Zach, who ran off to join Jason and Kylie, and we went into the trees to wait until the others returned.

CHAPTER 20

JARED AND I sat on the grassy bank next to the creek and he took something from his saddlebag.

"Is that where you carry your weapons?"

He chuckled. "We don't carry weapons. This is a portable CD player. We might as well listen to some tunes while we wait."

A thumping noise vibrated the air. Screeches and squawks in a kind of a rhythm came from the small case. Jared sat, eyes half closed, swaying and twitching his shoulders to the thumping beat. In a few minutes it was over and he glanced at me. "So, what do you think?"

"It sounded like a she bear with cubs fighting a puma."

Jared laughed. "At least you're honest. I guess that sort of music is an acquired taste. What kind do you like?" He flipped through some small shiny wheels. "Maybe I have something you'll enjoy."

"Well...Clemente, our vaquero, strums a guitar. I like

to listen to him sing and watch his wife dance. Over at White Wolf's pueblo the Indians beat on drums and play flutes."

"I have some guitar music you might like. This is Paco de Lucía one of the great guitarists from Spain."

I did not understand how the music came from the CD player but I did not ask. It sounded nothing like Clemente's guitar. The song, too, was new to me, but very pleasant. I nodded. "I like that."

"Yeah, I'm taking lessons and some day would like to play a guitar as well as he does."

We talked then. The Spanish came more easily to Jared, and I began to understand some of his language. Once more he reached into his saddlebag and pulled out a book. "This is a Spanish/English dictionary," he said. "If we have trouble understanding a word, we can look it up in this book."

Soon we were speaking in a combination of the two tongues, because, as he said, some words had no translation. I told him of my life on the ranch and he spoke of movies, television, malls, and automobiles. "I can't begin to tell you of the technology we have now that didn't exist even fifty years ago," he said.

I didn't ask how all these wonders came to be or how they worked. The knowledge would do me no good when I returned to my own place in time, and my brain was already crowded with the strangeness of this world.

After a while I said, "Enough time has passed. The others should be here soon."

He glanced at his bracelet. "You're right, but how did you know? You don't wear a watch."

"The position of the sun, the shadows it casts."

He tapped his bracelet. "This is a timepiece. It tells me each minute and hour of the day. How do you tell the time when there is no sun?"

I shrugged. "Even when clouds veil the sun, there is some shadow. The moon and stars have their own positions at various times of the night. The birds and animals tell us of coming storms, of the change in seasons. My body, too, tells me things when I take the time to listen to it."

I saddled El Cid and Jared took us out of the trees and to a hard-packed game-trail that he said led to the outside gate. We passed buildings that Jared said once housed the early Spanish settlers. None looked familiar. When we got to the gate, it was barred with a chain.

"You and I could climb over it," Jared said. "But what about the horse?"

I examined the wooden gate. "How high would you say this gate is?"

"Over six and a half feet, why?"

"I'm thinking that maybe he could jump over it."

"Isn't that a high jump for a horse?"

I didn't answer but climbed over the gate and examined the ground on the other side. It was smooth, with no rocks or grass, but hard as sandstone. If El Cid fell upon landing, he could hurt himself, and even if he didn't fall, he would jar his bones on the hard earth. I walked a few paces along the rock wall.

"Where are you going?" Jared asked.

"The wall is lower in some places and I'm looking for softer ground. If he jumps high enough, maybe he could—" I heard hoof-beats pounding on the hard ground and in the next instant El Cid sailed over the wall. He stumbled, fell on his knees, rolled over on his side, and scrambled to his feet. He snorted, shook his body, and limped to me.

I ran my hands over him, inch by inch. He flinched when I touched his shoulder.

"I've never seen anything like it," Jared said, his eyes large as his CD disks. "Is he all right?"

"I don't know. I think he hurt his shoulder."

"Here come the guys. We can get him to a vet right away if he needs it."

CHAPTER 21

FOR SOME TIME, I'd been aware of a low hum that gradually became louder. I looked up to see a huge machine roaring toward us. I must have looked startled because Jared said, "That's the automobile I was telling you about. It's pulling a horse trailer."

I stroked my trembling horse. I realized that everything was more frightening to him than to me. "It's noisy," I told him, "and it smells bad. But Jared assures me that it won't hurt us, and it will take us to the blue mesa swiftly. We'll be home soon."

The shiny red car screeched to a stop and Jason, Zach, and Kylie scrambled out. "You guys ready?" Zach asked. "I brought your horse like you said, Jared. Your dad asked all sorts of questions, but I told him we were going for a ride in the morning."

"We may have to take El Cid to a vet," Jared said. "You should have seen him." And he told them how my horse jumped the wall.

"What is a vet?" I asked.

"A veterinarian is a doctor for animals. He can fix El Cid's shoulder so that in no time at all he'll be walking without a limp."

"I'd rather go directly to the blue mesa," I said. "We can't take time for a doctor."

"Whatever," Jason said. "Let's get him loaded. It's getting late."

He opened the trailer at the rear and I was heartened to see it was only a wagon with a cover. El Cid limped badly when I led him to the trailer, and I remembered the rocky trail up the mesa. He could never make it to the top. I took him into the wagon and he seemed happy to see another horse.

"Snub him tight so he can't move," Jason said.

"He'll be all right," I said. "I'm staying right here with him."

"You can't. It's against the law."

"Why?"

"People aren't allowed to ride in this type of trailer. We'll get tickets, fines, I don't know what all, if the cops happen to stop us."

I didn't comprehend a word he said but had quit asking the meaning of everything. "Let's take him to this vet then." I climbed in the car. They shut the door with a bang and enclosed me in a small space with no visible means of escape. I could see out, but the opening was solid and slick to my touch. I forced myself to remain calm.

I sat in the back seat next to Kylie, so close my skin tingled pleasantly where our bodies touched. This sensation had happened to me before, but I couldn't remember the circumstances.

I forgot about the feeling, though, when the car growled. It settled to a steady hum and with a slight jerk moved forward. The seat beneath me vibrated and I glanced out the window. Trees, rocks, bushes sped past. Behind us, the museum grew smaller as we rolled down the path marked with a yellow line. The car swayed and Kylie leaned against me. Her scent made me dizzy.

"We're going around a curve," she said, and I smiled into her eyes.

Everything about this girl, from her blonde hair and blue eyes to her gentle touch, was familiar and somehow comforting.

The sun had dipped behind the mountains, but dusk had not yet settled over the land. "We're on the freeway now," Zach said. "Traffic is light this time of day."

Cars of all shapes and colors rushed past us, toward us, and around us. Monster cars—trucks, Zach called them—belched black smoke, roared, and shook the car as they passed us. Cars in the shape of long boxes crawled on the road. "Motor homes," Zach said. "Like houses on wheels. Some are extremely comfortable with all the modern conveniences."

The sounds, sight, and stench of all the cars speeding down the freeway overwhelmed me and I squeezed Kylie's hand.

She scooted closer to me and all too soon Jason pulled the car to a stop. "We're at the vet's. I'll talk to him while you guys take El Cid out of the trailer." When I didn't move, he showed me how the levers opened the doors. "But not while the car is moving," he said.

I backed El Cid out of the trailer and breathed a sigh of

relief when he appeared calm. Jared showed me where to take the horse so the vet, Dr. Black, could examine him.

"The horse looks healthy, what's the matter with him?" the doctor asked.

"He's a steeple jumper," Jared said, "and had a bad fall."

The vet moved his hands expertly over El Cid, but the expression in his eyes made me wary. "The jockey looks in worse shape than the horse. Has the boy seen a doctor?"

"Not yet. He's more worried about his horse."

"Well, the horse is fine. He only has a bruised shoulder. A few days of complete rest and he'll be good as new, but I'll take a blood sample just to be sure." Dr. Black took a wicked looking needle and plunged it into El Cid. "Now, young fellow, there will be no running or jumping this horse for at least three days."

"Three days? But I have to—"

He waved the blood-filled tube. "This horse is a fine specimen and it would be a crime to ruin him for life by forcing him to compete while he's hurt."

Jared took my arm. "Come on, Diego. Let's take El Cid home. Thanks, Doc, put this on my dad's bill."

"Leave the horse here," Dr. Black said, "so I can examine him further."

Jared hesitated. "Well, I guess that would be all right."

I shook my head. I would not be separated from my horse and did not trust the doctor.

"If the horse is all right," Zach said, "Why do you want to examine him further?"

"He looks to be of an ancient breed, and I'd like to make some tests."

"No!" I grabbed El Cid's reins.

"Well, I have a blood sample and can test it," the vet said. "Remember what I said, three days. Where will he be stabled?"

"At my house," Jared said and followed me out.

I put El Cid in the trailer. "I can't wait three days."

"I know," Jared said. "But maybe he'll heal sooner than that. We'll take him to my house. We have stables where he'll be comfortable, and you can stay with me."

We rode in the car for a while and Jason said, "There's Santa Fe over on your right. Have you ever been here?"

I could see no houses, but thousands of candles twinkled from their windows. "No, and I had no idea it was such a large village." Someone chuckled.

At Jared's house, he said, "My folks are out for the evening. You guys come back in an hour and I'll order a pizza."

We put the horses in the clean and warm stable. Jared filled a box with hay, and from a bin scooped out grain. Another trough held fresh water. "Come on," he said. "They'll be all right now, let's go in the house."

I took my blanket from the saddle. "I can sleep out here."

He shook his head. "Come in the house. I'll put medicine on your wounds, and no offense, but you could use a shower."

I followed him meekly, wondering how long it would take before my courage returned and I could exert my will.

We entered the house and more astonishing things attacked my senses. I paused in order to take in all the new wonders. What kinds of candles and torches were these that lit the house bright as a summer day? My brain whirled and I couldn't take everything in, so I followed

Jared up a flight of steps.

He paused at a door. "This is the light switch." A bright light suddenly filled the room, and I gasped in shock. Jared stood in front of me beside a dirty and bedraggled stranger. "We're looking in a mirror." He put an arm across my shoulders. "That's you. See what I mean about needing a shower?"

I had seen my image before, of course, in the still waters of a pool, in the polished steel of my sword, but never so clearly, and I'd never seen the color of my eyes. They were green, like Estrella's when she gets excited. I shrugged out of my tattered shirt and examined the ugly knife wound on my shoulder, the zigzag marks on my chest.

Jared laughed. "Okay. That's enough admiring yourself. Time for a shower. Here's soap and shampoo. Wash that yellow stuff out of your hair."

"It's tule, Apache magic medicine."

"Yeah, well I have some magic medicine that will heal you in a hurry."

I believed him. Everything I'd seen since I met him was magic. He showed me the shower and how to adjust the water temperature. More magic. I removed my boots and stepped under the warm spray.

"Um, Diego? You can take your pants off to shower."

"They're the only ones I have with me so thought I'd wash them."

"I'll loan you some of my clothes. Here's a towel to dry yourself. Call me when you're done, I'll be nearby."

I glanced down at the muddy water swirling around my feet and pulled off my buckskin trousers. I left them on the shower floor and poured shampoo on my head. White suds, red dirt, and yellow tule ran off my body and on to the trousers. I stomped on my pants, lifted them, and hung them over the door. The water ran out small holes in the floor and disappeared.

I stood under the shower until the water ran cold and Jared knocked on the door. "Diego? You about done?"

I shut off the water, stepped out of the shower, wrapped the towel around my body, and once more looked in the mirror. I hardly recognized myself. My hair hung dripping to my shoulders and my face was a harsher image of my sister. I touched my upper lip where a shadow of a mustache grew.

"Yeah, you do look a lot better," Jared said. "Sit down and I'll put medicine on your wounds." He spread a white ointment on my head and shoulder. "You never did tell us how you got injured. The others are already here, maybe you'll tell us while we eat." He bandaged the wounds with a sticky substance he said was a Band-Aid. It stuck to my skin without benefit of cloth ties.

He gave me what he called jeans, and a red shirt with a drawing of a wolf. Made of finely woven cotton, the shirt was soft against my skin.

"That's the symbol of our state university. We're called Lobos."

I traced the letters with my finger and memorized the words. Father Marcos always told me that I had a gift for languages, and that may have been the truth. Already I could say several words of this strange tongue and understood quite a lot more.

We went downstairs where the others waited. "You clean up really good," Kylie said. I didn't know what to answer so only smiled.

She handed me a string with two silver disks. "Use this to tie your hair back. It's a ponytail holder." I turned the string over in my hand. It had no end. "It stretches, see?" She pulled it into a large circle. "You put your hair in it like this...and there it is—a ponytail."

I had never thought of my hair as a horse's tail.

The pizza was a delicious wonder, and I devoured my share of the large tortilla spread with tomatoes, meats, cheese, and herbs.

At their insistence, I told my friends how Black Bear kidnapped Estrella and of our flight across the plains to the blue mesa. "So, you see, I have to return so I can find my sister and see her safely home."

"What of White Wolf?" Zach asked. "Won't he take Estrella home?"

"If he is able. But there is more. The Indians have already attacked our home, and I am concerned about my family."

"Do you all realize that we have history sitting right here beside us?" Jason asked. "You know, Diego, at first we thought you were a homeless bum. But you had a horse and that made us wonder. Now we see that you're not much different than us. In those clothes you even look like one of us. I guess people haven't changed much over the centuries. We have more technology than you, but that's all."

I glanced around the comfortable room and thought of the marvels that existed in this time—the magic lights, the ease of acquiring delicious food, the automobiles, the warm spray of the shower—yet I did not envy my friends. While they had all those comforts, I had the magic of a sunrise, the joy of the hunt, the feel of a horse between my legs, the taste of a cool mountain spring.

CHAPTER 22

THE NEXT MORNING, I awoke at daylight and without disturbing Jared went to the stables to check on El Cid.

I heard him snorting and pawing and I flung the door open. A man was attempting to put a halter on my horse's head.

I grabbed the man by his collar. "Leave my horse alone!"

He swung the halter at me. I caught his wrist, but the reins slapped my cheek a stinging blow. I grabbed him by the shoulders and held him against the wall. "What do you want with my horse?"

He stared at me, his brown eyes huge, his mouth worked wordlessly, and I realized he did not understand my language. I snatched a rope off the wall and bound him hand and foot.

I ran to the house and joggled Jared awake. "Come quick. I caught a man trying to steal El Cid." He pulled on his jeans, and we hurried to the stable.

Jared stared at the man thrashing helplessly on the floor. "You did this to him?"

"Ask him what he wants with my horse."

"He works for Dr. Black, the vet. Maybe—"

"Ask him."

They spoke too rapidly for me to follow and finally Jared said, "Dr. Black wants another blood sample from El Cid and sent this man to get it."

"Why didn't he tell us? Why did he try and steal my horse?"

"He wasn't stealing him. He said they just wanted to verify something about El Cid's DNA, and I guess Dr. Black didn't think you'd agree to bring him in for more tests." Jared grinned. "They didn't count on you waking up so early."

"Dr. Black will make no more tests on my horse. Tell his man that."

"All right. And we might as well untie him."

I stood with my arms folded across my chest while Jared loosened the knots. The man ran from the stable without a backward glance.

I took my saddle down. "I'm leaving for the blue mesa."

"The doctor said you should wait three days."

"I trust nothing that doctor says or does. He might send his man back here for El Cid."

Jared chuckled. "He won't be back. You frightened that man so bad I thought he'd...well, anyway you scared him, and to tell the truth, you had me scared too."

"How did I do that? I only wanted answers."

"The way you looked. The way you still look, with your

eyes blazing and that fierce expression."

"I'm sorry, and I thank you for all you've done for me, but I must go now."

"Have some breakfast first. Then we'll take El Cid to Zach's house. Dr. Black will never suspect where we've stabled him and that will give the horse a chance to rest one more day. Later this evening, we'll drive to the blue mesa."

I saw the logic to that and again gave in to his argument. At the house, I wrapped my buckskins in my blanket.

"What are you doing?" he asked.

"Where El Cid goes, I go."

He gazed at me with the same look Esteban so often gave me. "All right, but you're bleeding again. Put this on your cheek." He handed me the tube of ointment. "Keep it. At this rate you'll probably need it again." I put the medicine in my pocket.

His mother was in the kitchen cooking breakfast when we got downstairs. He introduced us, and she said, "What are you boys planning for this weekend?"

Jared told her we were taking the horses and going camping with the other guys. She nodded but seemed more interested in my blanket than in our plans.

"May I see your rug?" she asked.

I unrolled it and held it out. She took it and carefully examined each stitch. "This must be at least two hundred years old, maybe more."

"My mother is a docent at a museum," Jared said, "and has a real passion for old Navajo rugs."

"Surely you're not taking this camping," she said.

"It's my only blanket."

"Loan him a sleeping bag, Jared, this is too precious to take out in the rocks. Where did you get it?"

"My mother—"

Jared kicked my shin. "It's been handed down in his family for generations."

"Well, it has been well cared for and is in excellent condition. It's a wonderful artifact and belongs in a museum. Even the colors are still vibrant. Plant dyes usually fade over the years but see how bright the yellow is."

"They used yarrow for the yellow, and—"

Jared kicked me again. "Come on, the guys are waiting."

We left his mother admiring my blanket. Outside, he said, "We have to be careful. You don't want to be poked and prodded like El Cid or your blanket, do you?"

No, I did not want that. I had to leave this time and place soon. We saddled our horses and rode to Zach's house. We went slowly and El Cid did not limp. When we got to his house, Zach said, "Your mom just called. She said Dr. Black wants to take another look at El Cid and will be at your place in an hour."

"We won't be there," Jared said, and told him about the morning.

"Put the horses in the stable. While El Cid rests, let's get Jason and take Diego to the market at the plaza."

"I thought we were going to the blue mesa," I said.

"We are, but not until this evening, and you really should see Santa Fe before you go back."

Once again, they enclosed me in a car, but I liked this one better. It was yellow and had no top. I prayed that the wind on my face would return my lost courage to me.

We picked up Jason, and, in the village, we drove through streets teeming with people and cars. "Where do all these people come from?"

"Some live and work here, but many are tourists here on vacation."

What kind of work did they do? What were tourists or vacations? I did not ask.

The plaza was set up on the verandah in front of an adobe building. My friends told me it once housed the presidio. Vendors, wrapped in ponchos, sat on low stools or cross-legged on the ground, their wares spread on blankets. The tourists pressed around them, haggling over a turquoise ring, an obsidian pendant, or a silver bracelet. The noisy throng, the closeness of bodies, the odors, assaulted my senses. I longed for the stillness of the plains, the fresh air of the high mesas, the scent of piñon.

A shop, at the end of the long verandah, displayed tomahawks with colored feathers dangling from the handle, lances painted in bright colors, knives decorated with turquoise—weapons that no Indian I knew would use, either for hunting or battle. I entered the open door.

A large box, made of the substance I now knew as glass, stood in the center of the room. It held silver and turquoise objects. A small dagger in one corner caught my eye.

"May I help you, sir?" A woman asked. She had red painted lips and fingernails, eyes outlined with charcoal, and wore a short black dress that hugged her body.

"That knife there in the corner, the one with the turquoise and white handle."

She opened the glass box with a small key and

removed the knife. "You have a good eye. This is a fine piece of art. Hand-made by Navaho artisans right here in Santa Fe. A worthy addition to any knife collection." She handed me the knife.

I tested the shiny blade. "Navaho? It needs sharpening."

She took the dagger from my hands and replaced it the box. "One would never sharpen it, sir. It is for display only. Could I interest you in another, one that perhaps you would find more useful?"

I took my small knife from my boot. "I would like to make a trade for this one. The tip is broken."

She blinked. Her eyes turned cold and in a haughty voice said, "I'm afraid we cannot accommodate you. Perhaps if you went to a pawnshop..."

My friends entered the store. "What are you doing in here, Diego?" Jason asked.

"I'm trying to trade my knife for a different one."

Jared laughed. "They don't make trades in this store."

I remembered the silver ore. "I have silver." I reached in my pocket. The woman turned her back.

Zach tugged my arm. "Come on, let's get out of here."

CHAPTER 23

BACK ON THE street we faced the masses of people. Selling bundles of the sacred white sage, a man strode through the crowd with the bearing of a chief or a shaman. He wore his hair in two braids and his jeans tucked in knee-high boots. I peered at him closely. "Lame Deer! Is that you?"

His eyes widened. "No one calls me by that name anymore. Who are you?"

I grabbed his arm. "Look at me, Lame Deer. It's me. Diego Montez."

"It can't be." He studied my face. "But it is. Storm Cloud! How did you get here? The wind...what were you doing on the sacred mesa?"

"It's a long story. Lame Deer, I have to talk with you."

"Yes, you do. Come with me." He guided me away from the throng and into a quiet alcove of a large building.

My friends followed. "This is more exciting than

hanging out at the mall," Zach said.

"Sit." Lame Deer pointed to some wooden benches. "It is good to hear my name spoken again. Now tell me how you came here."

I told him everything. I even told him of my vision of Santiago saying, "Help your family," and of White Wolf's long-ago vision of riding the sky on a black horse through the rainbows. "What am I going to do, Lame Deer? I must get back."

"From what you told me of your vision, your destiny is clear," he said. "You must return and help your family."

"Will the wind on the blue mesa carry me home?"

"I know of no other way."

"Why did you never return, Lame Deer? Chief Leaping Antelope said you've been gone for two moons."

He shook his head. "As time is counted here, I've been gone for five summers."

"How is that possible?" My voice shook.

"Here, in this time, I've met many wise people and even learned to read. I have learned that what you and I experienced is called a time warp. That is why you are no older than when I last saw you, yet for me, many seasons have passed."

I glanced at my friends. They looked as stunned as I felt. How many other people had the wind taken to another place in time? And why had no one ever returned? "Lame Deer, will I ever be able to return to my own time?"

He sighed. "I don't know, Storm Cloud. Come, let's go to my house where we can talk in private."

"My friends know everything."

"Yes, they may come with us."

"We have a car," Zach said. "Just tell us where you

live."

At his house, Lame Deer led us into the kitchen. We sat at the table and his wife served us cinnamon cookies. They reminded me of those that Marta baked, and a wave of homesickness washed over me.

"I can never go back, Storm Cloud." Lame Deer made a sweeping gesture around the room. "This is my destiny. I, too, had a vision when I was young. A vision I thought would never come true. Yet here I am."

"So, if I have a vision, it will come true?" Jason asked.

Lame Deer gazed at him with the wisdom of five hundred years in his eyes. "If you want it badly enough, yes. We should all follow our dreams."

Even though I knew he might not answer such a personal question, I asked, "What was your vision, Lame Deer?"

He spoke quietly. "My vision was that one day I would be a great shaman. I never thought it would happen. Owl Feather is a powerful medicine man and taught me all I know. I was content with the Cucuri. Then, that day on the *Tsin* I prayed for peace and the wind brought me here. Now that I am here, I cannot leave. "

"Did you never try?"

"Yes. But I tarried too long and the wind wouldn't take me."

"But life here is so different. How do you manage?"

"I am a respected shaman. And I teach the young people the old ways so that our traditions will not be lost. That, too, is my destiny—to be a teacher."

"And my destiny is to save my family. I don't understand why that is so. My father is strong and brave, he has always protected us."

Lame Deer sighed. "The reasons are never shown to us, Storm Cloud. I only know what you told me of your vision and it was clear. You must go back to your own time and you must hurry. If you stay in this place too long, you may never get back."

Jared spoke up. "We're taking the horses and camping out at the mesa tonight. Diego thinks that the wind will return for him."

"Maybe...if you get to the mesa in time, and since you are here by mistake—" Lame Deer stopped talking, his eyes held a far-away look.

"You mean the wind meant to take me someplace other than here?"

"No, I mean the wind grabbed you instead of White Wolf and Estrella."

The idea astounded me. "How could that be? We both fought the wind. I just wasn't quick enough."

"You pulled them out of the whirlwind, Storm Cloud. They galloped down the mesa, you were behind them, and the wind took you instead."

I nodded, remembering. "White Wolf's vision. But the rainbows in his vision, what do they mean?"

"That is for Owl Feather to explain when you get back. But you should know, Diego-Storm Cloud, that when you do go back, the wind will not be denied. It will try and snatch White Wolf while he is riding his black horse."

My stomach clenched. My mouth went dry. If I stayed here, I would not fulfill my destiny. If I returned, the wind would take White Wolf and my sister. How could I make such a choice? "What should I do?"

"You must go back, that is your destiny, and you

haven't much time."

"How long do I have?"

"Twenty-four hours from when you were caught by the wind. If you get back within that period, it will be as though none of this happened. If not, you may never get back to your own time."

Each of my friends glanced at their timepieces. "Let's get going," Jason said.

"Wait." I held up my hand. "What can I do to save White Wolf and my sister from the whirlwind?"

"There is nothing you can do to save them, Storm Cloud. It is their destiny. I do not know, but perhaps White Wolf has a duty to perform in some other time and place. And there is something about the black horse that is important."

I pounced on that bit of information like a hawk on a sparrow. "Maybe if I tell White Wolf to turn the black horse loose, the wind will pass them by."

Lame Deer shrugged. "Maybe."

"Thanks, Lame Deer. I'm headed for the blue mesa now."

He nodded and rose from his chair. "Another thing, there is no guarantee that the wind will take you back to your own time. Still, you must try. A word of caution. Take nothing from this time with you and tell no one back home that you saw me. Good luck." He ushered us out the door.

CHAPTER 24

MY MIND REELED with all that Lame Deer told me. My friends sensed I was bewildered, and no one spoke as we climbed in the car and drove away. After a few minutes, Zach said, "Now what?"

"We don't have much time," Jason said. "We should stop for some food and then get the horses. We could go to Wal-Mart. It's on the way home."

The marketplace was more than my confused brain could manage. I stood by the door, but my feet would not move me forward. "I'll wait for you here."

Jared nodded in understanding. "We won't be long."

I gazed about and slowly my brain focused.

A pole, with brightly colored kerchiefs hanging from it, stood in the corner. My hat had disappeared in the whirlwind and I had no covering for my head.

A man said, "May I help you with something?"

"I'd like this red and white kerchief, please."

He took the kerchief and went behind some sort of desk. "That will be a dollar sixty-nine."

I stared at him. "I don't understand."

"What's to understand? You want the bandana? Pay me a dollar sixty-nine and it's yours."

"A dollar sixty-nine?"

"Yeah, give me the money and this red bandana is yours."

"I don't have money."

He set the kerchief on the desk behind him. "Then you don't get the bandana."

"I'll trade you something for it."

"Trade? This ain't no flea market, boy, this is Wal-Mart."

At that moment, my friends came to the desk. Jason was pushing a cart. "What's the matter, Diego?"

"You know this guy?" the man asked. "He wants the bandana but doesn't want to pay for it."

"Put it in the cart with the rest of this stuff," Jason said. "We'll pay for it. Our friend is from another country and doesn't understand everything."

The man turned friendly. "Oh, that's different. Will there be anything else?"

"No thanks." Jason handed me the kerchief. I wrapped it around my head and tied it at the nape.

"Come on," he said. "We better hurry. It's almost eleven. We have to be at the mesa no later than four."

At Jared's house, I changed into my own clothes but looked with longing at the red shirt. "Keep it," Jared said, and I put my torn shirt on over it. How could I repay my friends for all they did for me? I had only the broken pieces of silver ore. I reached into my pocket and handed each of them a chunk of silver.

"We can't take it," Zach said. "It's too valuable."

"It's from the magic cave. I want to give you something, and I can always get more." To me, their friendship and kindness was much more precious than a handful of silver ore.

We drove to the blue mesa in two cars. I rode with Jason in his red car that pulled a trailer with El Cid and another horse. Jared rode with Zach in a brown car they called a pickup.

I worried for the entire distance. Was I doing the right thing? What would happen to White Wolf and Estrella once I returned home? If I stayed in this century, would the wind spare them? Or would it take them at the first opportunity? And what of my parents, and the people of the hacienda? Would I reach them before the Indians massacred them? I found no answers and took comfort in Lame Deer's insistence that I must return home.

CHAPTER 25
2021 – The Blue Mesa

THE SUN WAS past the mid-day mark when we pulled off the freeway and onto dirt wagon tracks. "This is as far as we can drive," Jason said. "We go horseback from here on."

We saddled the horses and set off through clumps of sere grass and withered bushes. If not for the blue mesa looming ahead, I would not have recognized the area. We rode around the base of the mesa until we found the path leading to the top.

I turned to my friends. "This is where I leave you. Thank you for everything."

"We're riding to the top with you," Jason said.

"You can't. Suppose the wind takes you, too. You can't take that chance."

"I wouldn't mind," he said. "I'd like to experience your way of life."

I shook my head. "It's very different, and besides,

Lame Deer said there are no guarantees as to where the wind will take me."

"We hate to see you go. We'll probably never see you again," Zach said.

Jared glanced at his timepiece. "We still have a couple of hours left before you have to leave. I'll build a fire and we'll have something to eat before you go. We bought some hotdogs. I think you'll like them."

"Yeah," Jason said, "And I want to take your picture." He stood beside me and held up what they all called a cell phone. He stretched out his hand and said, "There."

"Ah, you took a selfie. You all stand next to El Cid," Zach said, "and I'll take your picture and then I want one of me with Diego."

He held his cell phone up. "There, we'll see your photograph in just a few minutes."

A small box spit a square of white paper, and we watched as a picture slowly appeared. I stared in amazement at my image standing next to my friends. Every detail on the paper was clear, even to the wolf on my shirt.

"I would like a picture of each of you to take back with me," I said.

They took turns snapping their phones until we had a pile of photos and Zach said, "Hold it. I don't have any more paper for the printer." Still, they took more pictures on their phones.

Jared gathered dried branches of the cholla cactus and built a fire. I watched in interest as he struck a flame. "These are matches." He showed me how they worked. "Keep them, I have plenty more." I shoved the small box into my pocket.

We admired the photos while we ate the hotdogs. My image was in each picture, some of me astride El Cid brandishing my sword, several of me with each of my friends. "I wish we could have figured out a way to take a good picture of the four of us together," Jared said.

We divided the photos among us and I carefully placed mine in the saddlebag. "I better get on my way." I was reluctant to leave my friends but knew I had no choice.

"Someone is coming." Zach pointed to a swirling dust cloud. "It looks like a Jeep, probably forest rangers."

Two men got out of the Jeep; one carried a shovel. "Don't you boys know that you are in a restricted area? It's against the law to have a fire out here."

"No," Jared said, "we didn't know. I'm sorry, but we saw no signs."

The man with the shovel piled dirt on our fire. "Well, you should have known anyway. It's been in the news on TV, newspapers, and the radio that fire danger is extremely high because of the long drought. Are those your cars and trailers at the edge of the road?"

Jared nodded.

"Get on your horses and away from this area. And I mean right now. Go home. No camping permitted until the fire danger is passed." The ranger poured water on the ashes. "Go on now, you kids. We are staying by this fire until not one spark remains. The wind is starting to kick up. It won't take much to get a prairie fire started."

"All right," Jared said. "But before we go, would you please take a picture of the four of us together? Our friend here is from another country, and we would like a photo of the four of us with the mesa in the background." He handed him his cell phone.

The Blue Mesa

The ranger laughed. "Sure. Stand close together. Smile. I'll take one on each of your phones."

The photos showed us standing with our arms around one another, our horses behind us. We gazed at the pictures, then at each other, our eyes bright with tears, and with sad smiles, nodded.

"All right," the ranger said. "Now get going."

We turned our horses toward the road. "How much time do I have?" I asked Jason.

"Fifteen, twenty minutes."

"Goodbye. Thank you again. I'll never forget any of you." I headed El Cid toward the mesa.

The ranger grabbed at El Cid's bridle. "Hey! What are you doing? Turn around! This is a restricted area."

"I have to get to the top of the mesa." I pulled back on the reins. El Cid reared, whinnied, and pawed the air.

The ranger backed away. "No one is allowed up there. Come back here."

I nudged my horse and he dashed toward the mesa. I turned my head. The ranger ran behind me, shouting. The wind snatched his words and blew them away. The other ranger jumped in the Jeep and chased me.

Apparently, this car didn't need a hard-packed road. It bounced over rocks and low bushes. Growling and squealing, the Jeep roared closer and closer.

"Hurry, El Cid, we haven't much time." I bent low in the saddle and he galloped up the rocky trail. I prayed that the path was too narrow for the Jeep. I didn't turn to look but concentrated on gaining the mesa top, and I didn't spare my horse.

At the top, I reined in El Cid and glanced around: at the lookout rock, the sandstone basin, the stunted trees.

Everything looked the same, yet different. The lookout rock seemed smaller, the sandstone basin deeper, the stunted trees shorter. Silence surrounded me, not a breath of wind stirred. At the foot of the mesa the wind had blown with a stinging force. Was I too late? For the first time, I envied my friends' timepieces that could measure the minutes and seconds.

The cave! Maybe if I entered the cave, I would awaken the wind. But a pile of boulders blocked the entrance. I picked up a rock and tossed it aside, then another and another. I pushed stones too large to lift, used a dried tree branch as a lever to move the larger boulders. A low moan from deep within the cave broke the stillness. Only the largest rock remained blocking the opening.

"Hey, kid! What are you doing? We told you this was a restricted area. Get away from that cave." The forest ranger ran toward me, scrambling over rocks.

I called on my patron saint. "Santiago!" Strength surged through my body and I heaved on the lever with new power. The last boulder moved. A blast of stale air hit my face. I pushed harder and released the wind. It shrieked out of the opening and knocked me to the ground.

"Get back. The wind is dangerous," the ranger shouted.

I dashed to El Cid and leaped into the saddle. The wind gathered force and with a loud howl, gyrated toward us. I soothed El Cid the best I could, we had to remain still so that the whirlwind could take us back to our own time.

The ranger wrapped his arms around a boulder. The wind took his hat, his shirt flew open and flapped around his head.

The wind screeched and twisted hard and fast, twirling around El Cid and me until it lifted us off the

136

ground. I peered through the swirling sand and caught a last glimpse of my friends. They were looking toward the sky and waving their arms.

I tried to see the earth as I whirled backward through the centuries but couldn't keep my eyes open against the strong wind, so I gripped the saddle with all my strength. My brain reeled. Was my timing right? Would I reach the mesa at the exact instant I'd left? Or would I land in some other place in time?

Suddenly we touched solid ground and the wind whirled off the mesa, sweeping away rocks and loose tree limbs as it continued its southward course.

CHAPTER 26
1680 – Home

I TOOK A deep breath and glanced around. The mesa looked as it did before the wind took me. On the spot where Black Bear and I had battled, bits of silver ore glittered in the sun. I gave thanks to my patron saint that I had arrived in my own time safely. But I couldn't tarry, I had to warn White Wolf of the wind. I prayed Lame Deer was correct and White Wolf was at the foot of the mesa.

I urged El Cid down the hill, and he was happy to obey. I wiped my sleeve across my eyes, but my arm was bare. My red wolf shirt was gone. I spotted my hat wedged in the branches of a stunted juniper. The wind returned the hat but took my shirt and red kerchief. I slapped the hat against my leg to brush off the dust, tied the leather thongs under my chin, and pulled the hat low over my eyes.

El Cid was nervous and pranced and bucked so I kept a tight rein on him. My heart lifted when I saw the black horse racing the wind with Estrella and White Wolf clinging to his back. "There they are, El Cid. Hurry!" The whirlwind twisted and turned until it closed in on them.

The wind howled and shrieked like the lost souls of purgatory and Guapo ran as though the demons of hell were chasing him. I nudged El Cid to a faster gait, but he balked the nearer we got to the whirlwind, so I dismounted and blindfolded him with my tattered shirt. The swirling sand shrouded my eyesight and pecked at my bare skin with angry bites. I held onto my hat with my free hand, bowed my head into the wind and led the horse through the storm.

Sudden silence enveloped me like a cloak. Not a blade of grass moved. The wind was gone and with it my sister and White Wolf. I squinted and wiped dust from my eyes, but Estrella and my friend were nowhere in sight. I searched for tracks, but the wind had swept the ground clean.

A large and beautiful rainbow arced across the sky. I removed the shirt from El Cid's eyes and rode on toward the rainbow, hoping to see them behind every rock or clump of trees. The rainbow led me on, fading slowly as I rode until it disappeared. The landscape yielded nothing but red rocks and dusty bushes. I scanned the heavens for the whirlwind. I saw nothing but blue sky.

I remembered what Lame Deer said about White Wolf's vision. An icy hand squeezed my heart when I thought of them galloping forever across the sky. Even Guapo couldn't outrun the wind.

El Cid snorted and pricked his ears. My chest tightened with disappointment when I saw that it was only the other horses. Bonita nickered, trotted to us, and with the other two horses, trailed behind us.

I concentrated on the search and wasn't prepared for the arrow that whistled over my head. I dug my heels into my horse's flanks and flattened myself across his neck. El Cid leaped into a full gallop and I prayed the Indians would be satisfied with the other horses and not pursue me. But the horses galloped with us, and, when I turned my head, I saw that the Indians were of the Navajo tribe. There were four of them, and they carried bows and arrows and lances tipped with broken sword blades.

I pulled my own sword from its sheath and looked around for a likely spot to stand and fight. I caught sight of a sandstone escarpment a short distance away, and I guided El Cid toward it. When we reached the rock tower, I wrapped the reins around the saddle horn and turned to face the enemy.

With wild yells, they raced toward me, brandishing their lances and letting loose arrows that missed me, *Gracias a Dios*. One warrior came at me with his lance upraised. With a shout of "Santiago y Montez" I lashed out at him and gored him in the stomach. He fell forward and I snatched his lance with my free hand. The memory of my vision gave me strength and I struck out at one warrior with my sword, then at another with the lance. I caught them by surprise and they fell back, but my war-horse was not done. He charged and, with their companion's lance, I knocked the Indians, one after the other, from their horses.

El Cid reared, whinnied, and danced on his hind legs, proud of his part in the short battle. I patted him on the neck and called him pretty names. He stomped his feet, snorted and tossed his head, accepting his due.

The Navajos gained their senses and gathered their

scattered weapons. I urged El Cid to a gallop and we fled from the battle scene. I was not surprised to see the Navajo ponies following me. None of these horses were far removed from the wild mustangs, and as herd animals, they prefer to be with their own kind. All the horses had apparently accepted Bonita as the lead mare and El Cid as chief stallion, for they followed wherever I led.

I remembered my promise to White Wolf. I had to abandon the search for my sister. The enemy was dangerously close to the ranch, and I was needed there.

I would have to trust that they had outrun the wind and White Wolf would bring Estrella home safely.But deep in my heart I was afraid. Afraid they had not escaped from the wind and I would never see them again.

With my small herd of horses, I loped toward home, this time with a watchful eye for the enemy.

CHAPTER 27

MY BELLY KNOTTED with anxiety the nearer I got to the hacienda. I prayed that I was wrong and that Estrella was already home. My spirits lifted when I saw the green valley. I looked down at the ranch buildings. All appeared peaceful and quiet, but there was no activity in the courtyard. The corrals were deserted, no hens scratched in the barnyard, and the thought crossed my mind that everyone had escaped to Santa Fe. I slowed El Cid to a walk, led my small herd of horses to the corral and shut the gate on them. As I unsaddled El Cid, Esteban entered the stable carrying a coiled reata.

"That's a fine bunch of horses you brought with you, Diego," he said. "Where did you get them?"

"They followed me," I said.

Esteban pointed to the brown and white mustang. "From the markings, this one is an Apache horse. These four belong to the Navajo. Here is Bonita and the other horse is White Wolf's." He eyed me with that appraising look of his. "You probably have quite a story to tell."

I shrugged. I had no story to tell, only that I had failed in my mission. "Where is everyone?"

"In the guard tower. We've been staying there the past few days. It's safer."

Gaspar came into the stable, a wide grin on his face. "You're back Don Diego, and I see you brought the señorita with you." He pointed to Bonita.

I shook my head. "No, Gaspar. I wasn't able to bring her home."

"But these horses..."

"He says they followed him," Esteban said.

I didn't understand why they were so interested in the horses; we had plenty of our own. "What has been happening around here?" I asked.

"The Indians came," Gaspar said. "We drove them off, but they stole our livestock. All that is left are two yokes of oxen, a couple of swine, a milk cow and a few chickens."

"They took all our horses?"

Esteban nodded. "The only horses we have now are these you brought with you. We will need them for our flight to El Paso del Norte. I'll wash the war paint off them and give them grain and water."

"You're going to El Paso? Why?"

"We are all leaving, Diego. We only waited this long for your return. All the Indian servants left the hacienda days ago."

Panic seized me. We could not leave the ranch without Estrella. I had to talk with Owl Feather. "Where is Chief Leaping Antelope?" I asked.

Gaspar lifted one shoulder. "He should be here in a day

or two. He is to lead us around the Indian war camps."

"I have to talk with Father." I dashed out of the corral and to the house.

I stopped outside the kitchen door and took a deep breath before I walked into the house. My mother was at the fireplace, her back to the door. "Madrecita?"

Mother turned around; her face wreathed in smiles. "Diego!" She ran to me and hugged me tight. She peeked around my shoulder.

I shook my head. "Where is Father?"

Her face fell. "I'll get him." She went out into the courtyard. "Rafael," she called, "Diego is home."

Father strode into the house with a happy grin. My shoulders sagged and my stomach dropped. I knew what I had to say would erase all joy from my parents' lives. He clapped me on the back and said, "It's good to have you home, Son."

There was nothing more to do. I couldn't put it off any longer. "Mother, Father, sit down." I pulled two chairs out from the table and straddled a third.

"What is it, Diego?" asked Father. A worried frown creased his brow. Mother crossed herself but didn't say a word.

"Remember what Chief Leaping Antelope told us about Lame Deer? And Owl Feather said that a wind probably carried him away?" Father nodded. They both watched me intently but didn't speak as I told them about my adventures in the twenty-first century and how the wind took Estrella. When I finished, they still said nothing, only stared at me with disbelief. This was not the reaction I expected, but I understood. If I had not lived through that experience, perhaps I would not have believed it.

Finally, Father spoke. "What you're saying is that Estrella ran off somewhere with White Wolf."

"No, he got caught in the whirlwind too."

"You know that is an Indian myth. There is no wind in a cave that carries people away."

How could I make them see the truth? Lame Deer asked that I not tell anyone I had seen and talked with him. The wind had stolen my red shirt and kerchief. The photographs! I could show them the pictures of my friends. "Wait. I have proof that the wind took me to the twenty-first century."

I ran to the stable and rummaged through my saddlebags. The photos had disappeared; only a white powder remained. The wind had stolen all reminders of my friends and left me with only my memories. Dejected, I returned to the kitchen.

"It's all right, Diego," Mother said. "We love White Wolf, too. I know he will care for Estrella and treat her with love and respect."

Father stood. "Come help me, Diego. We have to pack as much food and gear as the carts will carry. Leaping Antelope and his warriors will arrive at first light to guide us past the war camps."

"We can't leave here yet," I said, my voice louder than usual. "We have to wait for Estrella." Then, although I knew I hadn't the right, I told them of White Wolf's vision.

Mother reached out and touched my head. "You've been wounded, Diego. Come let me put some healing salve on it."

Madre de Dios, they thought I was hallucinating. I shook my head and sighed. "I'm all right."

But Mother brought warm water and I sat slumped in

the chair while she tended to my wounds. The Band-Aids had disappeared. She combed my hair and held up the two silver disks from the ponytail holder. "What are these?"

What had happened to the stretchy substance? "They are decorations from the ponytail holder my friends gave me."

Mother shook her head and clicked her tongue. She washed my hair and declared the wound had healed. "How did you get this?" she asked as she dabbed ointment on the knife cut on my arm. "And this?" She pointed to the zigzag scar on my chest. "And your shirt is nothing but a rag."

I shook my head and said nothing. I would speak no more about my adventure and the attempted rescue.

"You look tired," Father said, his voice soft and concerned. "Rest awhile on your bed. Sleep if you can. Things will look better to you after some rest."

My entire body suddenly ached with fatigue. I went to my bedroom and lay down. I closed my eyes and the room whirled. Weariness overcame me and I sank into sleep.

CHAPTER 28

IT WAS DARK when I awoke. I didn't know if it was morning or night and I lay on my bed thinking. Maybe I had dreamed that the whirlwind whisked me far into the future and then brought me back only to take Estrella and White Wolf. But it was all so clear—my friends and all they did for me, the foods I ate, especially the pizza. And how could I have dreamed the wonders I saw in the twenty-first century: the cars, the stores, the magic lights?

I knew everything else had happened: our escape from the Apache camp, Estrella's sprained ankle, my fight with Black Bear, White Wolf coming to the mesa—all of that was real. But if the whirlwind hadn't taken them, where were White Wolf and Estrella? I could find no answer.

I arose from my bed, found my tinderbox on the table and lit a candle. Someone had brought in hot water, probably Marta. I scrubbed myself and donned clean buckskins, brushed my hat, and pulled on my other pair of boots. I took the little knife from the old pair and ran my thumb over the nicked blade. It needed honing. I remembered what the haughty woman said when I tried to exchange it. I never did discover what a pawn shop was. All that could not have been only a dream. I placed the knife in my boot and stepped out into the courtyard.

People seemed to be everywhere. Father came up to me. "Leaping Antelope will be here soon, and we must be ready to leave. Pack what you want to take with you."

I looked around the familiar surroundings: the goat shed where both Estrella and I learned to milk goats, the storage room where, when I was eight years old, I'd found a large bull-snake curled in the hollowed-out log we used as a grain bin. I'd chopped its head off with a hoe and Father scolded me for that. "*Never kill a harmless creature, Diego. A man kills only for food or to protect himself and his family. The bull-snake lived on the mice and rats that stole the grain. Now I need to find another to take its place, and you are going with me.*" Together we searched under rocks until we found the brown bull-snake that still lived in the grain bin.

These and other memories, some happy, some sad, crowded my mind. "Why are we leaving our home, Father?"

His eyes filled with sadness. "If it was only you and me, Diego, I would stay and fight, but I must think of your mother and the people of our hacienda. They would stay and fight with us if I asked, but I cannot do that. Already we have lost some. An Apache arrow killed old Pedro. Clemente was badly wounded when he and Manuel were returning from taking the horses to the canyon. The governor has fled to Mexico with all the troops and we, the people of New Mexico, have no protection. Entire families have been massacred and haciendas wiped out. Without the soldiers, we cannot succeed in a war with the Indians. They are determined to drive all Spaniards out of the territory."

A chill ran down my spine as I remembered my friends telling me that the Pueblo Indians had won this war, killing those Spaniards who had not escaped to El Paso, and a sense of urgency swept over me. I had to find Estrella soon.

Father placed a hand on my shoulder. "We have a responsibility, Diego, you and I. We must see to it that our people are protected at all costs. Even if we must leave Estrella here in New Mexico, even at the expense of our own lives, we must never forget our obligation. Our people rely on us, Son Diego, and I am proud that you are fighting by my side."

A wave of guilt washed over me. I'd been thinking only of myself. Past the lump in my throat I said, "I'll go pack, Father. It won't take me long," and returned to my bedroom before he saw the tears in my eyes.

I didn't need much. I'd take only what I could carry in my saddlebag. I rummaged through the pockets of my old buckskins and found the small box of matches. Relief swept through me and weakened my knees. I sat on my bed and struck a match against the sandpaper strip on the box. Instantly a flame flickered, and I watched it burn down to my fingers before I blew it out. Here was proof that I had visited the twenty-first century. I stroked the box and the English words: "Strike Anywhere Matches". I knew the words only because my friends from the twenty-first century had explained them to me.

I could show the matches to my parents and prove I had visited the future. But what purpose would that serve? They still might not believe me, and it was enough that in my own mind I knew I had not dreamed my adventures. I reached in my pockets once more and pulled out the tube of ointment Jared had given me. More proof. I smiled to myself and with a lighter heart rolled my clothes in a blanket. I'd get another knife from Gaspar. I had yet to apologize to him for losing his musket. I looked around the room, there was nothing more I needed. I blew out the candle and went out into the courtyard.

I stopped at Estrella's room and stared at the closed door. I pushed it open and stepped inside. I had no hope of ever seeing her again and wanted a memento of my sister. At her desk I lit a candle, picked up the pages of her journal and stuffed them inside my shirt. They would fit easily in my saddlebag. I glanced around one more time and my eye caught a familiar bundle on the bed.

My chaps! And Estrella's ragged skirt! I picked up the chaps and examined them closely. They were my chaps. The ones I'd given Estrella at Black Bear's wickiup. And that was her skirt. I thanked the saints she was alive and had not been caught by the whirlwind or captured by enemy Indians. But where was she? If White Wolf had brought her home, why weren't they here? He had promised to bring Estrella home, and White Wolf always kept his promises. My head whirled and I sank into a chair. Maybe the rap on my head had scrambled my brain. I held my head in my hands and tried to clear my mind. I don't know how long I sat there before I again remembered White Wolf's vision.

The black horse touched ground for a moment before

racing off into the sky again.

Estrella and White Wolf had been here. I didn't know
how and I didn't know when. Maybe while I slept, maybe
just a few minutes ago. But they had been here, and they
might come back. I had to talk with Owl Feather. I ran out
into the courtyard.

The place buzzed with activity. The oxen stood yoked
to carts that were piled high with supplies and tools.
Perched on top of the baggage were cages made of reeds
that held chickens and ducks. A milk cow tied behind one
of the carts calmly chewed her cud.

The Navajo horses were hitched to two wagons heaped
with sheepskins and blankets. These apparently would
carry the sick and wounded, the women and children. The
horses were not trained to harness and snorted and kicked
at the traces. We had a long trip before us, but an
experienced driver would have these horses pulling as a
team within five leagues or less.

El Cid stood saddled and waiting. I stroked his nose
and talked to him, then tied my blanket on the back of the
saddle and placed the journal in the saddlebag.

A lookout shouted from the guard tower. "They're
coming. To arms, to arms."

My heart leaped. At last, I would have a chance to talk
with Owl Feather. But it was not the Cucuri who rushed
down the hillside of our valley. A different tribe of the
Pueblo Nation attacked us with a barrage of arrows. With
leather slings they tossed stones that struck the tower with
loud thuds. Some had firearms and the musket balls
splattered against the guard tower and sent bits of rock
flying.

I took up a post at one of the windows where a bow

and a stack of arrows lay ready. At each of the small windows, men shot at the enemy with muskets or arrows. My skill with the bow and arrow was not what I'd like, but I pulled with all my strength and was heartened to see a warrior topple from his horse. Next to me my father's gun blasted and found its mark. Smoke and the scent of gunpowder lay thick in the guardroom.

Several of the enemy lay dead or wounded on the green hillside and the Indians carried them into the trees. There they dismounted and ran toward us shouting taunts, waving lances, throwing rocks, and shooting arrows.

"If we could steal some of those horses, we could move faster on our trip south," Esteban said in my ear. "What do you think?"

I liked the idea. The horses were probably some of ours anyway. "We can do it, but they may have a guard posted."

Esteban grinned and flashed a machete. "I'll take care of the guards. You get the horses."

At the munitions pile I shoved a knife in my belt, picked up a hatchet with a flint blade, and told Father our plans. "Be careful," he said. "Go behind the stables, through the draw to the bull pasture and around the trees. I'll post a lookout, and when you're at the pasture I'll shoot the cannon and we'll send a steady stream of musket balls and arrows at the Indians."

Esteban and I ran to the stables and at the draw, crouched low. When we heard the cannon boom, we ran to the forest and silently slipped behind trees until we saw the horses. They were tethered in the usual fashion—in a string of ten on a rawhide rope. A guard held one end of the line. He paid no attention to the horses. He was interested in the battle.

Esteban gave me a sign and we crept to the horses. I held the end horse by the halter, patted him and talked low. Esteban sneaked behind the herd and with one slash of the machete, the guard fell to the ground in a silent heap. Esteban took the lead-rope, and we led the horses through the trees. At the edge of the forest, we each leaped on a horse and galloped across the pasture. Arrows flew around us, but we were too far away and they did not harm us.

At the stable, Esteban picked two of the sturdier horses and hitched them to a wagon. They bucked and kicked but we managed to get them to the courtyard. We left the others as they were, with the Indian saddles which were little more than a sheepskin or woolen blanket tied on with a rawhide strap that had loops for stirrups.

CHAPTER 29

AT THE GUARD tower, we climbed the ladder to take up our posts. Gaspar met me at the top, and I was startled at the look of anguish on the old soldier's face. "What is it, Gaspar?" I asked.

"Don Rafael has been wounded."

My limbs went weak. I felt empty and drained. My hands fell to my sides. My legs wouldn't work. "Where is he?" I finally managed to croak.

"Here." Gaspar pointed. My father lay on his back, an arrow deep in his right shoulder. Gaspar knelt by his side. "Diego is here, Señor." With his scarf he dabbed at my father's face.

Father lifted a limp hand and beckoned. I knelt and leaned to hear. "Take our people to safety, Diego. They depend on you."

I clasped his hand. "Yes, Father. I promise." He closed his eyes. I bent my ear to his chest and was relieved to hear his heart beat with a steady thump. "Shouldn't we take the arrow out, Gaspar?"

"Yes, but the arrow is deep and it will be very painful." He sat back on his heels with such an expression of grief on his face I knew he didn't want to remove the arrow. I understood. I didn't want to do it either, but it had to be done.

"The Cucuri are coming," Esteban shouted, and the sound of battle dimmed.

I peered out a window. Chief Leaping Antelope rode a horse painted with red and black war symbols. Flanked by two war chiefs, he led his small band of warriors down the grassy slope. The enemy Indians retreated to the trees. Chief Leaping Antelope stopped and talked with them, then rode up to the gate undisturbed.

Gaspar lifted my father to his feet and together we carried him to the opening in the floor. There, many helping hands guided him down the ladder to the lower level.

My mother gasped when she saw him but immediately called to Marta and directed the men to lay my father on a sheepskin on the floor. By this time our Indian friends had crowded into the tower and the old chief called for Owl Feather.

From a pouch made from the scrotum of a bull buffalo, the medicine man took a powder, mixed it with water and forced the liquid down Father's throat. Father coughed and spat, but he swallowed most of it and fell back on the sheepskin. In a short while he was asleep.

Owl Feather broke off the shaft of the arrow at the feathered end and tapped the shaft with his knife blade until the arrowhead came out the other side. Then he placed a foot on Father's back and, with a grunt, pulled out the arrow. His flesh tore and Father moaned and twitched in his sleep. With a sharp cry Mother fell to her knees and sopped up the blood that flowed from his wound like a spring freshet.

After Mother bandaged his shoulder, four men picked Father up and laid him in the wagon where a bed had been prepared next to Clemente. Mother climbed in the wagon and sat with Father's head in her lap. Gaspar took up the reins and hopped onto the wagon seat.

"We must hurry," Chief Leaping Antelope said. "We have only a short time before the enemy returns with reinforcements."

"Get everyone started, Esteban," I said. "You lead, I'll ride flank." I watched as every member of the hacienda climbed in wagons or on horses and followed Esteban out the gate of our home.

CHAPTER 30
Leaving the Hacienda

THE CUCURI WARRIORS formed two lines that stretched from the gates of the courtyard to the hill. Our wagons and horses filed between the Indians. When he passed, I stopped Owl Feather. "I must talk with you."

"We don't have much time. We can talk while we ride."

"No, I must talk with you now, here at the ranch." I told him what had happened to Estrella and White Wolf.

"Yes, that is what happens when people go to the sacred mesa. I warn them, yet they insist on making the trip."

"But they didn't get caught by the wind on the mesa, Owl Feather, and they did come back to the ranch." I told him about my chaps and Estrella's skirt.

His eyes showed fear. "That is not possible. No one has ever come back from that mesa."

"I did. And they did. How else did my chaps get here?"

"Even though the wind didn't take them from the

sacred mesa, it was very angry and chased them until it caught them."

My heart sank, yet I couldn't ignore the fact that Estrella and White Wolf had been here at the hacienda. "You made medicine over Estrella's pendant. What kind of magic does it hold? Could it be the necklace that saved them from the whirlwind?" Once again, I related White Wolf's vision.

"White Wolf had a vision?" He fingered his medicine pouch and thought for a moment. "The wind took them, there is no doubt about that, but the stone is blue and that's what brought them to earth. Your sister wears the stone so she is protected. White Wolf is not wearing blue. If they both wore blue, they would be anchored to the earth. But as it is..."

I remembered what Lame deer had said. "What about the rainbow in White Wolf's vision. What does that mean?" I'd pondered that question a hundred times but couldn't find the answer.

"Is not your sister's Indian name Rainbow? And in his vision didn't White Wolf carry a blue bundle?"

"Of course, that's the answer. Thank you, Owl Feather. And to keep them here on earth, White Wolf needs to wear blue?"

"Yes. Your sister could stay if she'd leave White Wolf."

I knew she would never leave White Wolf. "Catch up with the rest. I'll be along shortly." I hurried to Estrella's bedroom and rummaged through her clothes until I found a blue kerchief. A pot with a wolf design held a blue ribbon and some blue beads. I put these in a pile on her desk.

I took a clean sheet of paper and dipped the quill into the ink. I wrote:

Dear Estrella and White Wolf,

I talked with Owl Feather. He tells me that since you were taken by the whirlwind, in order for you to stay anchored to the earth in this time and place you both must wear blue. I know you returned to earth once, and Owl Feather says that is because you have the blue sapphire pendant. I pray you will return once again. Here are some blue articles for you to wear. I am in a rush as we must leave our home until the Indian trouble is resolved. I shall return to the ranch as soon as it is possible.

May God and the saints bless and protect you.
Your brother, Diego

I had to hurry to catch up with my people. I loped out of the gate and turned for one last look at my home. An arrow whined over my head and fell harmlessly to the ground. I pressed El Cid to a gallop. My place was with my people and their flank was unprotected.

I heard an explosion and again turned. The stables and chicken coop were on fire. The flames climbed high, red and yellow tongues lapped at the dry piñon poles, and I feared the tanning shed, blacksmith shop and other buildings would be destroyed. I could do nothing to save our ranch, so I galloped on.

At the top of the hill, I turned for one last look at my home. A column of smoke blackened the air. The stench of scorched pelts and smoldering manure stung my nose. I rubbed a hand across my eyes. I told myself that it was not tears I wiped from my face, it was sweat from the heat of the flames and odor of our burning ranch.

Chief Leaping Antelope posted lookouts along the way and led us through arroyos and around outcroppings of rock. We rode without stopping for about three leagues before he halted the caravan. "I leave you now, my friends. Keep riding south and you should be safe."

"Thank you, Chief, for your help. I know that it is dangerous for you to side with us." I extended my hand.

"You and your father are the only good Spaniards I know. You have never shown cruelty to us. Your hacienda has shared your food in times of famine. Your father is an honorable man. He has kept his word to us for all these years." The Chief gazed at me with an intent look, sadness and the wisdom of his years showed in his face. "Make no mistake, Storm Cloud, we are not friends of the other Spaniards. We go now to join forces with our own people. I have spoken with the other chiefs of the Pueblo Nation, and the people of your hacienda are free to leave our territory. If you continue to travel southward, you will not be harmed."

He and his warriors turned their mounts and we were left on our own.

CHAPTER 31

THE RESPONSIBILITY TO lead our people to safety weighed heavily on my heart. My father lay severely wounded in the bed of a wagon. My mother wiped his feverish face with a wet cloth and said prayers. With a grim face and hard eyes, Gaspar drove the wagon. There was no one I could ask questions; all our people looked to me for answers.

I spurred my horse and galloped to the head of the file where Esteban rode White Wolf's horse.

"The Indians have set fire to the stables, Esteban, and they are not far behind. I don't know how much longer we can keep this pace."

Esteban looked at his wife Sage, who was riding next to him on Bonita. Esteban raised his eyebrows in question. She nodded. "We'll be safe, Diego, as long as we keep riding south. Chief Leaping Antelope gave his word."

"Do you think it will be safe to rest the night at the

mission?"

Again, Sage nodded.

Dusk was deepening when we reached the mission. Only the adobe walls remained. Broken adobe brick and smashed pottery lay in the shadows. Small animals scurried through the tumbleweeds piled in the corners. An owl flew on ghostly wings across the sky. I searched for the priests. On the altar, Father Marcos lay impaled with a lance, his face a distorted mask of agony and terror. The holy man had not died quickly, nor had he died well. Beads from his broken rosary lay scattered in the dirt. There was no sign of Father Anselmo, his assistant.

I built a fire and no one noticed how quickly I struck a flame with my matches. While Sage prepared a meal, we lit torches and in the flickering glow of their light, Esteban and I dug a grave in a corner of the courtyard. The dry, packed earth resisted our efforts and sweat trickled into our eyes and down our necks. Even though I was sweating, a cold lump settled in my stomach, and I blamed it on the cool evening breeze that swept through the courtyard stirring little whirlwinds of dust.

We had no material for a coffin, so we wrapped the priest in a woolen blanket and I covered his face with my neckerchief. I called for my mother. She left my father's side with reluctance but she, too, knew her duty. She knelt beside the grave with the other women and led them in reciting the rosary. The men stood with bowed heads, hats in hand and muttered the responses. We shoveled dirt over the mangled body of the good padre— my teacher, my mentor. My eyes filled with water and my vision blurred. I found the wooden cross Father Marcos used in the Processional during Sunday Mass. It was broken at the base, but I pounded it into the dirt at the head of his grave. The mournful howl of a wolf sounded far to the west. The first star of the evening twinkled in the darkening sky.

I gave orders for the care of the stock and assigned guards armed with muskets to patrol the inside perimeter of the mission walls.

After a quiet meal, I sat before the fire and thought of my twin sister, Estrella. I prayed that all was well with her and pulled her journal from my saddlebag.

Rebecca came and sat beside me. I smiled into her blue eyes and she snuggled against me. My body stirred at her softness and I pulled her closer. She reached up and with light fingers caressed my cheek. Then, gentle as the touch of a butterfly wing, her lips brushed mine.

My heart skipped a beat and I put my arms around her. The journal papers crinkled between us and fell to the ground. I kissed her eyes, her cheek, her lips. I paid no heed when the wind ruffled the journal papers and some of the pages fluttered away. Rebecca placed both hands on my chest and gently moved away. "I have to help my mother," she said. "Read the journal if you like. I'll return in a few minutes."

My hand trailed down her arm and I kissed her palm. "Hurry back."

I picked up the scattered papers and tipped them closer to the campfire to better read the thin scratches of my sister's handwriting. I smiled at the ink blotches and read the first pages of her journal...

After I finished reading, I rolled the papers and returned them to the saddlebag. I walked around the camp. My father was resting with my mother beside him. The people of our hacienda were settled for the night. I talked with the guards. All was as calm and peaceful as the silent stars that twinkled above us. A coyote yipped his evening song and a chorus answered.

I returned to my place by the fire. Rebecca waited for me and I gathered her in my arms. She lay her head on my shoulder and for a long time we stared into the yellow flames without speaking.

After a bit, I told her of finding Estrella's skirt and my chaps.

"They did escape the whirlwind, then," Rebecca said.

"They must have arrived at the ranch while everyone was in the guard tower before the Indian attack. I'm surprised no one saw them, though."

"Remember, the attack before that last one, the one where the Indians stole all the horses and Pedro was killed? There was no one to take his place guarding the fields, so if Estrella and White Wolf came the back way, we wouldn't have seen them from the guard tower."

I remembered how quiet the hacienda appeared when I'd arrived home. I had thought the place deserted.

"If Esteban hadn't gone to the shed for some rope, he wouldn't have seen you, Diego. Everyone was busy in the guard tower preparing to leave. We'd already packed all the food. That's why there was no one in the house." Rebecca clasped her hands around her knees and stared into the fire. Her hair gleamed like burnished gold. "I do hope they're safe," she said.

"White Wolf pledged to never leave Estrella. He is strong and a good hunter. He will protect her." I was relieved to learn they had escaped the whirlwind but was not convinced I'd ever see them again.

Rebecca placed her small hand on my arm. "Try not to

worry, Diego. I must get some sleep. I'll see you in the morning."

After Rebecca left me for her bed, I began to write the story of my sister, Estrella, and my friend, White Wolf, and of our people who were forced to flee their homes.

An owl hooted in the dark. The coyotes began their nightly serenade. I lay the quill aside and huddled under my blanket.

CHAPTER 32

I AWOKE TO a hand shaking my shoulder and Gaspar's voice. "Wake up Don Diego."

My eyes flew open. The sky was already bright, but my eyelids were heavy. "Sorry, Gaspar. I overslept."

"It's Don Rafael." His voice cracked.

Instantly alert, I threw the blanket aside and strode to my parents' wagon.

My father lay on the sheepskin, his skin was gray, his face gaunt, and his lips drawn back in a grimace. Mother sat with his hand clasped to her breast, eyes cast to the heavens, and her lips moved in soundless prayers. "He is worse this morning," she said when she saw me.

I bent my head to his chest. His heartbeat was steady, but faint. "Have you looked at the wound this morning?"

"The color is not good," she said. "To keep the flesh from rotting, it is necessary to cauterize the wound."

I looked at Gaspar. His eyes were filled with anguish.

He shook his head. "I cannot do it Señor."

There was no one else. I had to be the one to sear my father's flesh. "I'll need a hot fire and a branding iron." I remembered what Jared had said about keeping a wound clean to prevent infection. "And heat some water."

Gaspar stoked the fire and brought a poker from one of the carts. One such as I'd used many times to trace our brand, an M, on a cow's hide. He shoved it into the blazing embers, and I walked around the camp while I waited for the iron to get hot. I refused food when someone offered it. I kept my mind focused on the task at hand. Sweat trickled between my shoulder blades and my palms were wet.

When the iron burned red, I directed the vaqueros to hold my father down. "Sit on him if you have to, but do not let him move." My voice sounded gruff and strange to my ears.

I grasped the red-hot branding iron and prayed the saints would hold my hand steady. I took a deep breath and thrust the glowing iron into the gaping wound. Putrid tissue hissed and with a shivered scream, my father jerked and bucked. He gave a small moan, and then lay silent, unconscious from the pain.

I stepped back, the odor of burned flesh sharp in my nostrils, the echo of my father's scream resounding in my ears. Weak and drained, I dropped the iron.

Father lay limp and ashen. Sweat beaded his brow. Mother dipped her fingers in a jar of ointment. I reached in my pocket and brought out the medicine Jared had used on me. "Use this on the burn," I said. "It works almost like magic."

She examined the tube with suspicion. "Where did you

get this?"

"My friend from the twenty-first century used it on my wounds."

Mother dropped the tube as though it burned her hand. "If you went there, it was the work of the devil. I will not use it." She dabbed her own salve on the burn and bound it with a clean cloth. "He can rest easy now," she said.

"At least keep the wound clean with hot water."

Her eyes wide with horror, she said, "I can't wash him. Sick as he is, he'll take a chill."

"No, Mother, it will help prevent infection." I picked up the tube and replaced it in my pocket. Maybe later I could convince her that this was a good healing herb and would help my father. I gazed at my father's pallid face and my hand trembled as I stroked his brow and smoothed back his hair.

A soft hand touched my arm. "You had to do it, Diego. You probably saved his life."

"Estrella! Where did you come from?"

"We got here a few minutes ago. I've been talking with Gaspar. He told me what you did."

"Did the wind take you? I've been so worried."

"I have a lot to tell you, Diego. Things you will never believe, but first I want to see Papa." Estrella walked over to the wagon and took Father's hand in hers.

I sat on the wagon tongue, my head in my hands. Gaspar brought me a much-needed drink of water and then left me to my thoughts. My brain was so filled with all that happened the past few days, I thought my head would burst. Where had Estrella and White Wolf been? Would Father recover? Could I lead my people to safety?

I don't know how long I sat before I remembered what Lame Deer told me about the black horse. I found White Wolf hunkered on his heels by the campfire. His blue shirt shimmered like the summer sky at mid-day. "Don't ride Guapo, White Wolf." I told him of my experiences with the whirlwind. "Lame Deer said that the wind wanted you and the black horse."

"We escaped the wind once, Diego, and we're far from the sacred mesa. Surely we are no longer in any danger from the wind."

"White Wolf is right," Estrella said. She and Rebecca sat beside the fire with us. It was like old times—the four of us together, talking, except that we lacked the easy laughter, the sense of peace and security.

"Remember the story of El Dorado that old Pedro told us so often?" Estrella asked. "Cibola really does exist. White Wolf and I saw it. The rainbow took us there."

"But White Wolf said the wind didn't catch you."

"It wasn't the wind," Estrella said. "It was the rainbow."

"I saw the rainbow after the windstorm died. I tried to ride through it but it disappeared. Tell me what happened to you."

"You believe us then. We didn't think anyone would. Diego, it was beautiful. We were racing the wind and the rainbow suddenly appeared. Guapo galloped through it and a village appeared, with buildings made of gold, doors encrusted with jewels and the streets glittering with shiny stones."

"Were you able to bring anything back with you?" I asked, remembering how the wind had taken away my wolf shirt.

"Only my dress."

For the first time, I noticed her skirt. It was made of silk in the soft colors of the rainbow and sprinkled with twinkling stars. "Where did you get it?"

"My skirt was in tatters, remember? The rainbow ended in front of a golden church, and we were met by a man in shiny clothes and wearing a tall hat with a cross on it. He said we were in the first of the seven cities and that we were destined to visit all seven but couldn't in our rags. He waved his hand and my skirt changed to this beautiful dress and White Wolf's shirt to that one of shimmering blue."

"But I found your other clothes and my chaps at the ranch. How could that be?"

Both Estrella and White Wolf widened their eyes in surprise. "I don't know," Estrella whispered. White Wolf shook his head.

"Did you visit the other cities?" I asked.

"No. The rainbow appeared again and somehow we ended up here."

"Then hopefully the danger is over."

"What about you, Diego?" Rebecca asked. "Would you like for the wind to take you back to the future?"

"There is no need for me to return now that I know Estrella and White Wolf are safe."

"But what of your friends and that blonde girl who gave you the pony-tail holder?"

"I would like to see my friends again and learn from them all the wonders of the twenty-first century, but my place is here."

"Did you find her pretty?" Rebecca asked.

Pretty? Why did it matter? It seemed Rebecca had the

power to confuse me. "I suppose so." I tipped her chin, looked into her blue eyes and smiled. "She reminded me of you. Come on. The sun is high. It's time we got on the trail."

CHAPTER 33

I GAVE ESTEBAN orders to prepare to leave. "A visitor is approaching," he said.

A man leading a burro trudged toward the mission. His cassock flapped around his bare legs, and we recognized him as the missing Father Anselmo. I thanked the saints he was alive and had not been tortured. Swords at the ready, Esteban and I walked out to meet him. He raised his hand in greeting when he saw us. His clothes were tattered and dusty. We escorted him down the road to the mission.

"Where have you been?" I asked him. "What has happened to you?"

"I've been doing missionary work among the Pueblos," he said. "And I met with nothing but failure. Even at some of the more friendly pueblos, women pelted me with stones, men threatened me with knives, and children set dogs on me. It was very discouraging."

"How long have you been away?" I asked.

"Not more than four weeks and never have I been so happy to see the mission. At some pueblos I barely escaped with my life." Shock paled his face when we entered the mission gates. "What has happened here?" he asked.

Esteban and I told him about the rebellion and showed him Father Marcos' grave. Father Anselmo dropped to his knees in prayer. We left him and turned our attention to packing the wagons.

Estrella ran up to me. "Papa is awake, Diego, and wants to talk with all of us."

I hurried to his wagon and was grateful to see that father's eyes were open. "Isabella, my love," he said, "I have failed you. I pledged to make this country a safe home for you and our children. I am sorry I was unable to keep my promise."

Mother patted his cheek. "You have given me a good life, and we are not yet done. We have years ahead of us. I have no remorse."

Father gave her a faint smile. "Diego, I am proud to call you son." His voice was weak and thin.

"Thank you, Father. We will get on the road now if you feel well enough to travel." I tried to keep my voice steady.

"Yes, we must keep moving. Don't worry about me. I want to talk to you about Estrella and White Wolf. Where is White Wolf?" He looked around; his eyes were dark and feverish.

"Hush, *querido*," my mother said. "Don't fret yourself."

"White Wolf is here, Papa."

"Diego," Father said, "You must lead our people to safety, but with White Wolf's help Estrella will stay and work the hacienda until you can return. Give me your hand, Star." Estrella placed her hand in his and with great effort, Father brought it to his lips. "Bless you, my little Star. And you, White Wolf."

Estrella bent and kissed his wan cheek. "Thank you, Papa. I pledge to keep the hacienda in good working order, and if it's God's plan, you will soon be home."

"Go then, both of you. We must all be on our way." Weak from the effort of speaking, Father sank exhausted on his pallet.

Mother pulled Estrella and me away from his hearing. "You cannot do this, Estrella. You must not live with a man you are not married to."

"I have to obey my father," Estrella said. "Owl Feather will perform the marriage ceremony."

Tears stood in our mother's eyes. "I would not rest easy, my daughter, knowing your marriage was not blessed by the holy church."

"Are you willing to marry my sister by a priest?" I asked White Wolf.

He said yes, and I went in search of Father Anselmo.

I found the friar lying prostrate on the grave of Father Marcos. I pulled the priest up by his collar. "You are needed," I said.

"I can do nothing," he said. "If not for me, Father Marcos would be alive. I left him to face his suffering alone."

"If you had been here when the Indians came, you too would by lying under a mound of clay. There is nothing to be gained by blaming yourself for the death of that good man. It is the living who needs your help."

Father Anselmo dusted his knees and wiped sweat from his brow with his sleeve. His pinched face was streaked with dirt. "What is it you want of me?"

"We need you to perform a marriage."

"I cannot do that. I haven't the means." He gestured toward the ruined mission church. "I don't even have any holy water."

"All you need to do is say the words and bless the couple. Come, we cannot linger here at the mission. The Indians may return at any time."

Father Anselmo followed me with grudging steps but brightened when Mother greeted him with delight and dropped to her knees for his blessing. He frowned again, though, when he saw the marriage couple. "I cannot sanction a wedding between an Indian and a Spaniard."

Esteban drew his sword. "Why not?" he asked, and I remembered that his marriage to Sage had not been blessed by a priest.

Father Anselmo shuffled his feet and fumbled with his beads. "How can I be sure the Indian is baptized in the true faith? At every pueblo I visited, people had scrubbed themselves and their children with soap plant to purge the baptismal waters from their bodies. Nothing I said or did swayed them from their heathenish actions."

"None of that has anything to do with White Wolf," I said. "Just say the words, Father Anselmo, so we can leave here. You can travel to El Paso with us if you like, there is nothing further you can do here."

At Mother's urging, and his eye on Esteban's drawn sword, the priest finally agreed to perform the sacrament at the altar of the church. The image of Father Marcos pierced with a lance was strong in my mind, so I persuaded the friar to bless the marriage outdoors in the courtyard.

Marta draped her white scarf over Estrella's head for a veil. I stood beside White Wolf and Rebecca stood next to Estrella. The friar led the couple in their vows, and after a few short words, blessed them, and then plodded off to the destroyed church chanting prayers.

"This is not the wedding I had dreamed for you, Estrella," Mother said, "but now I can rest easy. Be happy, my daughter."

Estrella embraced Mother and kissed her cheek. They hugged and murmured and kissed again. Marta stood next to Mother, tears streaming down her face. Estrella kissed her. "Take care of Mama until we are together again. I depend on you, Marta."

"I will, I will." Marta sniffled and sobbed into the end of her shawl. "*Vaya con Dios, mi hija.*"

Estrella turned to me. We neither one said a word. Her green eyes were bright with unshed tears. Finally, I grabbed her and hugged her tight. "Take care, little sister."

She nodded and wiped a tear from her cheek. She embraced Rebecca. They kissed, murmured something and smiled at each other. Gaspar handed Bonita's reins to Estrella. "Here's your horse, Señorita." Then he grinned. "I should now call you Señora."

She clasped him around the waist. "Oh, Gaspar." He helped her mount. "Diego," her voice broke.

I nodded. My throat was tight, I couldn't speak. Wordlessly, White Wolf and I clasped wrists. They turned their horses north and trotted away.

A rainbow suddenly appeared in their path and as I watched, White Wolf and Estrella rode through the arch and vanished. With a sinking feeling, I wondered where the rainbow was taking them and if I would ever see them again. Then I remembered that they were safe from the wind and the rainbows since they both were wearing blue. My friends from the future told me the settlers returned to their homes after twelve years. But I shall return before that time.

They also told me that many people who spoke their language lived many leagues to the east. I shall order a Spanish/English language book such as the one Jared had and learn the English language. Someday perhaps I shall travel there.

I checked on Father several times throughout our journey south. He was resting, and Mother assured me that in time he'd completely recover. Toward nightfall, we made camp in a deserted mission. Startled at our presence, bats swarmed from the bell tower and faded into the dusk.

After our meal, I sat by the fire and wrote more of our story, but it will not be finished until we Spaniards have reclaimed our ranches. So, I made this solemn vow: when I have seen my people to safety, I shall return to New Mexico, the place of my birth, and help bring peace to our land.

And Estrella? I do not know where my sister is but have hope of seeing her when I return to our home.

> Sealed,
> Diego Francisco de Montez
> The 25th day of August, in the year
> of Our Lord 1680

CHAPTER 34
2021

JASON AND ZACH met Jared at his mother's museum. "My mother told me about this, but I thought we should see it together," he said.

"What are we looking at?" Zach asked.

"Remember Diego's blanket? Well, my mother really liked it and Diego forgot about it when we left the house in a hurry that day."

"What about it?"

"She was all concerned when Diego didn't come back for his blanket, so I told her that he meant for her to have it. Anyway, she was so happy that she brought it to the museum and displayed it under glass to keep it safe."

The three boys walked into the museum, past ancient Indian clothing, clay pots, and flint arrowheads. Plastic figures demonstrated everyday life in an Indian pueblo. Prominently exhibited on the wall was a faded woolen blanket.

"That's Diego's blanket," Jared said.

Jason peered at it closely. "It can't be. This one is old and washed out. His had bright colors."

"I know. That's why my mom had the blanket authenticated by an expert. He said the wool was from the ancient four-horned sheep, and judging from the weaving, was at least four hundred years old. That was on Monday and already it had started to fade. Diego left on Saturday."

"Weird."

Zach laughed. "That ranger didn't say a word when he came down from the mesa with his hat missing and his shirt unbuttoned. I bet they never mention to anyone that we had even been there."

"Yeah, and I want to show you guys something," Jason said. "Sit down over here."

They sat on a padded bench facing the displayed blanket. Jason brought out his pictures. "Look at these."

"Are those the ones we took at the mesa?"

"Yeah."

"Where's Diego?"

"That's just it. Where is he? The one with the four of us together, there is just a blank space where he stood next to us. Even his horse doesn't show, this one is just a picture of the mesa."

"Let me see that." Jared peered at the picture closely. "There's a... Look. There where Diego should be, you can see a faint outline."

They studied the pictures one by one. Diego's image had disappeared from each, only the hint of his shadow remained.

"Let's go talk to Lame Deer about this," Jason said.

Lame Deer seemed pleased when they showed him the

pictures. "Of course, his image has disappeared from the photos. Diego himself belongs far in the past, but when you took his picture, you captured a piece of his spirit. Guard it carefully. He was able to take only his memories of you back with him."

Jared dropped his head.

"What is it?" Lame Deer asked.

"I gave him a few things to keep."

Lame Deer shook his head. "I told him to take nothing back with him. It would only cause trouble. What did you give him?"

"A shirt, ointment, a box of matches. I don't know, maybe some other things."

"What kind of trouble?" Zach asked. "He took a bandana with him too."

Lame Deer sighed. "It is never good to go against nature. It is one thing for him to leave something here in this time because it was made years and years ago and possibly could have survived. But for Diego, this is the future and the things you gave him were not yet invented back in his time and could change the course of history."

"What will happen?" Jason asked.

"I don't know." Lame Deer sat silent for a moment. "It will depend on how Diego uses what you gave him. Maybe the worst that will happen is that he will one day return to this time."

"I hope he does," Jason said. "He's one cool dude. I'd like to see him again." The other two boys nodded in agreement.

EPILOGUE

BY OCTOBER 1680, of the 2,800 Spaniards who had lived among the Pueblo Indians, nearly 2,000 reached El Paso del Norte. About half of the remainder were known dead; the rest were missing. Spain had experienced other Indian rebellions during her almost two centuries in the New World, but never such a devastating outburst of Indian fury.

Having chafed under the domination of the Spaniards, the Indians now suffered under the tyranny of one of their own. Popé, the hero of the revolt, declared himself governor of all the pueblos, and all were forced to pay tribute in goods and services. By the time Popé died in 1688, the Pueblo Nation was weaker than it had ever been.

In August of 1692, Don Diego José de Vargas led a military expedition to begin the reconquest of New Mexico. His force consisted of fewer than 200 men, only 60 of whom were Spanish soldiers; the rest were Indian allies, servants, and friars. Without firing one shot, spilling one drop of blood, or costing the Spanish crown one copper, de Vargas restored the territory to Spain.

The Spanish settlers returned to New Mexico and re-established their haciendas among the now peaceful Pueblo Indians. Yet, for the next two centuries, New Mexico remained untamed, and the Spaniards lived by the sword and the gun, the lance and the bow. Their survival hung on a precarious balance of power between Spaniard and Indian.

A proud and independent people, the New Mexicans proved able masters of their own fate.

THE END

AUTHOR'S NOTE

This is a work of fiction told against the background of the Pueblo Rebellion of 1680.

I have fictionalized the Cucuri Pueblo of the Tewa. To my knowledge no Pueblo by that name ever existed. However, many pueblos were destroyed during that war and their inhabitants scattered.

The Southwest abounds with legends of the Blue Lady, who some believe still roams the area bestowing love and riches on the deserving and causing blue flowers to bloom where she steps. The segment where the Cucuri connects the Christian legend of the Blue Lady to the Tewa Blue Corn Woman is a figment of my imagination. Likewise, I have exaggerated the whirlwind that exists on the sacred mesa of Tunyoh.

ABOUT ATMOSPHERE PRESS

Atmosphere Press is an independent, full-service publisher for excellent books in all genres and for all audiences. Learn more about what we do at atmospherepress.com.

We encourage you to check out some of Atmosphere's latest releases, which are available at Amazon.com and via order from your local bookstore:

Twisted Silver Spoons, a novel by Karen M. Wicks

Queen of Crows, a novel by S.L. Wilton

The Summer Festival is Murder, a novel by Jill M. Lyon

The Past We Step Into, stories by Richard Scharine

The Museum of an Extinct Race, a novel by Jonathan Hale Rosen

Swimming with the Angels, a novel by Colin Kersey

Island of Dead Gods, a novel by Verena Mahlow

Cloakers, a novel by Alexandra Lapointe

Twins Daze, a novel by Jerry Petersen

Embargo on Hope, a novel by Justin Doyle

Abaddon Illusion, a novel by Lindsey Bakken

Blackland: A Utopian Novel, by Richard A. Jones

The Jesus Nut, a novel by John Prather

ABOUT THE AUTHOR

Olivia Godat was born and raised on a cattle ranch in southern Colorado. Although she has made her home in the Pacific Northwest for many years, the unique history of the American Southwest still fascinates her. She has written several novels on the subject. She says the quote: "You can take the girl out of the country but you can't take the country out of the girl," perfectly describes her.

Made in the USA
Middletown, DE
21 November 2021